It was in th  Z struck for the second tim s what seemed to have ha feet halfway in when I realised that the shoes at least an inch too short. Jenks and Barney were sitting opposite, so I simply put my football boots back on.

I looked more closely at the shoes. It was a classy job alright. They must have swapped them for another pair. I'd guessed that much. Even so, they'd disguised the new pair perfectly. They'd copied the scuffing on the left toe exactly; and the broken right lace, too.

I turned them over. The letter Z had been carved into the soles with a penknife. I tossed them into my gym bag and, without a backward glance, walked out of the changing room. By the time I got home, my studs were wrecked, but a plan was forming in my head.

I had Agent Z sussed.

# MEETS THE
# MASKED CRUSADER

# MARK HADDON

RED FOX

AGENT Z MEETS THE MASKED CRUSADER
A RED FOX BOOK 0099712717

First published in Great Britain by The Bodley Head Children's Books, 1993
First published by Red Fox, 1994

This Red Fox edition, 2003

3 5 7 9 10 8 6 4 2

Copyright © Mark Haddon, 1993

Red Fox Books are published by Random House Children's Books,
61–63 Uxbridge Road, London W5 5SA,
a division of The Random House Group Ltd,
in Australia by Random House Australia (Pty) Ltd,
20 Alfred Street, Milsons Point, Sydney, NSW 2061, Australia,
in New Zealand by Random House New Zealand Ltd,
18 Poland Road, Glenfield, Auckland 10, New Zealand,
and in South Africa by Random House (Pty) Ltd,
Endulini, 5A Jubilee Road, Parktown 2193, South Africa

THE RANDOM HOUSE GROUP Limited Reg. No. 954009
www.kidsatrandomhouse.co.uk

A CIP catalogue record for this book is available from the British Library.

Printed and bound in Great Britain by
Cox & Wyman Ltd, Reading, Berkshire

This book is dedicated to Julian

Something Horrible Under the Duvet

# Something Horrible Under the Duvet

The boat was rolling and pitching in the heavy sea. I looked up and saw foam smashing against the glass of the porthole. Every now and then, as we were thrown to the top of a wave, I caught sight of the islands and the fat storm clouds hanging over them. I gripped the metal sink and stared into the mirror.

My face said it all. There were bags under my eyes. There was a long cut on my right cheek. My hair was everywhere. I was exhausted.

We had been anchored here for two weeks looking for the treasure. Somewhere, beneath the boat, was the wreck of the *Tornado*. On board the *Tornado* were the five hundred gold bars she had been carrying when she went down. We were going to bring them up to the surface. We hadn't come all this way to go home empty-handed.

It wasn't easy. For a start, we were surrounded by coral reefs. Last week the ship had drifted onto one, tearing a gash in the hull. We had to spend two days mending the hole to prevent her sinking.

There were sharks, too. Only yesterday, I had been diving with Captain Walker, searching amongst the coral for any sign of the *Tornado*. Suddenly, without warning, a shark the size of a submarine slid out of the darkness and ate him alive in front of my eyes. I escaped to the surface only in the nick of time.

To make things worse, the weather was going crazy. This morning, we had been sitting on the deck in blazing sunshine, planning our next dive. By lunch time, how-

ever, the sky had turned black, rain was hammering on the decks and the whole reef was caught in a typhoon.

I was dog-tired and I was seasick. I desperately needed to get some sleep, but I didn't know if it was possible in a storm like this. I splashed my face with water and towelled it dry. Stepping through the hatch, I made my way down the narrow corridor towards my berth, steadying myself against the walls as we heaved up and down on the monstrous waves.

'Are you all right, Ben?' It was Mum. She was standing on the landing, watering one of the rubber plants.

'Sure . . . fine,' I spluttered, taking my hand off the wall, standing up straight and walking into my bedroom.

I'm always doing that, imagining I'm somewhere else, drifting off into a world of my own. I suppose it's the reason I never watch much TV. It's like having a TV inside my head. Mum says it shows I've got a fertile imagination. She reckons it means I'll grow up to be a writer, or an artist, or something like that. Which is just like Mum. She always looks on the bright side of things.

Unlike Dad.

Drifting off into a world of your own drives Dad up the wall. I remember one night, a few weeks ago, I was lying in my room thinking about being a Viking when Dad put his head round the door. 'Ben!' he said, with a weary look on his face. 'What on earth are you doing? I've been calling you for the last five minutes.'

I said sorry and got up off the bed. But he wasn't going to let me get away with it that easily. He was standing in the doorway giving me one of his serious looks. 'Well?' he

3

asked. 'Why didn't you hear me?'

'I was being a Viking,' I explained.

'Honestly, Ben! You spend half the time with your head in the clouds. You've got work to finish for school. You've got a hundred other things to do. Your supper's going cold and you're miles away in Never-Never Land again. Why do you do it, eh?'

'I don't know, Dad,' I said.

It sounded really stupid. I don't usually have trouble answering questions. But when Dad starts looking serious, I get embarrassed and want to finish the conversation as quickly as possible.

'Go on, dream-boy!' he said, shaking his head. 'Get downstairs before your gravy freezes over.'

I thought about Dad's question later on that night. And when I thought about it, I knew exactly what the answer was. I knew *precisely* why I drifted off into other worlds.

It's like this. Some days, life is brilliant. The sun's out, lessons are a doddle, there's football in the afternoon and Barney, Jenks and I can spend the evening together in the park.

Other days, life is O.K., but nothing special.

And some days, life is the pits; and what you'd really like to do is just stay under the duvet with a hot chocolate and a packet of biscuits and not come out until the next morning.

The problem is, you can't decide what sort of day it's going to be. But if you close your eyes, it doesn't matter what sort of day it is. You can decide to be leading an expedition across the Sahara Desert. You can pretend to

4

be a scientist living in a space colony on the moon. You can look out of the window and imagine that you're wearing a jet pack, step off the sill and roar away over the factory roofs towards the hills.

So, why not? It doesn't harm anyone else. Sure, your supper gets a bit cold occasionally. That's alright. I can take hard gravy.

And why should it irritate Dad? After all, Mum goes brain dead watching soap operas, and he gets all dreamy listening to old rock and roll LPs while he's fiddling with the car.

Soaps. Rock and roll. Vikings. It's all Never-Never Land. They're just as bad as I am. It's just that when you're a grown-up you can get away with what you like. You make up the rules as you go along.

I decided that I should tell Dad all this. I'd answer his question in a really sensible and adult way. Then he wouldn't think I was quite so stupid after all.

But I never did get around to telling him. I didn't have the guts, for one thing, and I reckoned it would just have ended up as one of those really embarrassing, far-too-serious conversations.

I let it go.

When I got into my bedroom, after I'd bumped into Mum on the landing, I took off my dressing gown and hung it on the antlers Dad had screwed to the back of the door. I set my alarm clock and went over to take a look at Presley before I got into bed.

Presley was an African toad I'd got from the pet shop three years ago. He lived in a large, glass tank under the

Viking wall chart. I'd christened him Presley after Elvis Presley, the old rock and roller that Dad's a fan of. Like the real Elvis, Presley the toad started out looking slim and healthy and moving in a really funky way. Then he got old and fat and ugly and stopped moving altogether. Like the real Elvis, everybody thinks he's dead but, every now and then, there are reports that he may still be alive.

In the Congo, he would have eaten insects, but I gave him a tin of cat food once a week, and he seemed happy enough with that. I put a saucer of the stuff in front of his mouth, and shovelled away the droppings from behind him. He didn't need much looking after.

Recently, he hadn't been eating much. It wasn't worrying me. After all, he only moved about once every six months, so he didn't need the energy. Still, I made a mental note to ask Dad to take him to the vet if he was still off his food at the weekend.

It was when I slipped into bed that I noticed something was wrong. I thought it was grit at first, or jammy toast crumbs. All sorts of rubbish ends up under the duvet. I couldn't be bothered to get up and shake the sheet out, so I kicked it all to one side, put the Walkman on and started to doze.

Which was when they started to move – round my ankles, up my legs and between my toes. I ripped the headphones off, pulled my feet up and threw back the bedclothes. There must have been a hundred worms in the bed, muddy and pink and having a whale of a time. I threw open the window and breathed in big draughts of cold air to stop myself throwing up.

When my stomach calmed down, I walked out onto the landing and down the stairs. Mum was sitting in front of the television. She had changed into her luminous, green housecoat and had got her curlers in. She looked like something from the Planet Epsilon.

'Mum?' I interrupted.

'Sssh! Hang on a tic, love.'

She was watching the 1,248,635th episode of *Love Hotel*. She watched it every Thursday night. If Dad and she were going out, she recorded it on the video and watched it the next morning just to make sure she didn't miss anything important.

Now don't get me wrong. Mum's a brainbox. She learnt Spanish when we went to Spain. She can do my maths homework standing on her head (though she won't). And Dad refuses to play Trivial Pursuit with her because she's gone and won while he's still trying to think of the capital of Burkina Fasso.

She's a gas, too. Nothing ever seems to get her down. Even when I do something really moronic, like dropping one of the dinner plates when I'm doing the drying up, she just bends down, starts picking up the pieces and says, 'You're not going to play cricket for England, are you?' But when she's watching *Love Hotel* it's as if someone has taken her brain out. She's a soap junky.

So, I shut up, sat down next to her on the sofa and waited for the thing to finish.

On screen, Brad Piston, the owner of the Love Hotel itself, is standing in his marble and gold-plated office. He has a suntan and a moustache and is looking down at the city out of his twentieth-storey window.

Suddenly, the office door bursts open and in charges this unshaven tramp with a limp and mad-dog eyes. There's a burst of horror music and the camera zooms in for a close-up of Brad Piston's face. He's terrified. There are beads of sweat breaking out all over his forehead.

The tramp lurches over to the huge, leather chair on the other side of Brad's desk, sits down and hisses, 'Good to see you, big brother.'

'But Ernie,' gasps Brad, 'you're . . . you're . . . you're meant to be *dead*!'

The tramp leans over the mahogany desk, right up to the camera lens. He laughs wickedly. You can see the dirt in his wrinkles. You can almost smell his coat. 'I'll be staying in the penthouse suite, if that's O.K. with you,' he grins. Slowly, he stands up and begins to lurch back out of the office. 'Tomorrow, you can treat me to a slap-up meal and we can talk about the old days,' he announces, pausing before he slams the door and disappears.

Brad bangs his fist on the table and the screen goes all hazy. He's having a flashback. He is remembering a car accident many years ago. On the hazy screen, you can see Brad crawling away from the wreckage, leaving his younger brother trapped inside. He knew that his brother was in mortal danger, but he did nothing to save him.

So, Ernie has come back for revenge, etc., etc.

Brad's flashback finishes and he collapses into his chair with his head in his hands, a broken man.

When the credits came up, I said, 'Mum?'

'What is it, darling?'

'Have you been in my room today?'

'Only to get your socks and put them in the wash.' She took another liqueur chocolate from the box on her lap. 'I wouldn't forget *them* in a hurry. I sometimes think you soak them in manure, secretly, when I'm not watching.'

'Has anyone else been in my room?'

'I don't think so,' she mused, offering me a chocolate. 'You can have anything except the Cognac ones because they're my favourites, O.K.?'

'No thanks. I've already done my teeth.'

Dad appeared through the front door. There was oil on his face. He was carrying a broken headlamp and a monkey wrench. 'What's this, then?' he said, looking at me. 'You still up?'

'Have you been in my room today, Dad?'

'No.' He wandered through to the kitchen, put the headlamp on the bread board and began washing his hands. 'But Jenks and Barney dropped by.'

'Really?'

'Yep. They said you'd got some reading lists from Mr Lanchester for them, and could they take them from your room. You were out walking Badger at the time, so I told them to go right ahead. Why? Anything the matter?'

'Er, no. Nothing,' I said. 'That's O.K. Anyway, good-night.'

'Night-night, cherub,' said Mum, winking at me.

I wandered back upstairs.

I shook the worms out of the window, saving a few dead ones for Presley's saucer. Then I slipped along the landing, took a clean sheet from the airing cupboard and put the dirty one in the linen basket. When I lifted the wicker lid, however, I noticed a small piece of card lying on Dad's Y-fronts at the top of the pile. I picked it up. It read:

'GREETINGS FROM AGENT Z'.

# Schoolboy from Planet Zong

On Friday morning I was a hyper-being from Planet Zong, in the Xyr Galaxy. The Xyr Galaxy is on the outer edge of the Fourth Dimension. You won't have heard of it. You won't have heard of it because people on the planet earth know almost nothing about the rest of the universe, whereas we in the Xyr Galaxy know pretty much everything. That's because we're hyper-intelligent. We had time-transporters before you'd even got around to inventing the bus.

There were, however, a few things we didn't know much about. One of those things was the planet earth. We hadn't bothered, really. After all, the planet earth isn't *that* interesting. Nevertheless, I was working for a newspaper called the *Xyr Herald* and we were doing a series of articles about primitive people. So, I was spending a few weeks on the planet to see what the place was like.

It was a cinch of a job. The only problem was keeping my real identity a secret. I mean, if anyone ever found out that Ben Hurst was really a hyper-being from the Fourth Dimension, then I'd end up spending all my time doing TV interviews and being tested in laboratories.

I had to blend in. The school uniform helped. I left my tie loose, allowed my socks to sag round my ankles and kept the shirt buttons tightly closed over my three bellybuttons. I looked every inch a genuine human schoolboy. I thanked my lucky stars I'd taken a camou-flage class at the Xyr cadet college.

I cut across the recreation ground and climbed the gate into Melton Street. On account of my X-ray vision, I was able to see through the walls of nearby houses. There were people stealing from the biscuit tin, people going to the toilet, people talking to their cats in idiotic voices when no-one was looking. But I kept my eyes fixed ahead of me. I didn't want to give the game away.

Ahead of me, a green Fiesta pulled up at the kerb. Mrs Phelps was getting dropped off at school by her husband. I turned my head and my ultrasonic hearing picked up the squelch of his lips as he kissed her on the cheek. She hopped out onto the pavement, shut the door behind her and the car pulled away. As it did so, I noticed a strange sound coming from under the bonnet. Back in the Xyr Galaxy, we had built our own petrol engines in play school at the age of three. So, I knew instantly that something was wrong with this one.

'Hello Ben,' said Mrs Phelps, juggling with a pyramid of books and files. 'You're good and early.'

'Good morning, Mrs Phelps,' I replied. 'Can I give you a hand?'

'Very kind of you,' she smiled, loading me with eight copies of *The Age of the Dinosaurs*. 'Phew! That's better.'

'By the way,' I remarked, as we walked towards the main doors together, 'I think one of the spark plugs isn't firing properly in your husband's car.'

I wouldn't have said that to anyone else. When most teachers talk to you, you have to snap out of whatever you are thinking straight away. But Mrs Phelps made you feel relaxed. She was always interested in you. You could be yourself with her.

'Really?' She raised her eyebrows. 'The things you boys know about cars! I'll mention it to Geoffrey. Thank you.'

'Not at all,' I said.

I found Barney and Jenks hanging around by the corner of the science block. It was difficult to tell whether they were smirking when I approached, so I decided to play it cool.

'Agent Z!' I shook Barney's hand. He gave me a blank look.

'What's he on about?' Jenks asked.

'Just testing,' I replied, offhand. 'How was the film?'

'Eight out of ten, I reckon,' said Barney.

'Aaaiieeee. . . !' screeched Jenks, retracting into a kung fu crouch. Down on his haunches, he revolved slowly, then sprang to his feet, kicking out viciously with his foot.

Unfortunately, his foot collided with the briefcase of Mr Lanchester who had just walked round the corner.

'Are you mad, boy?' he asked, stepping backwards a pace.

'Sorry, Sir,' Jenks apologised.

'*Return of the Killer Samurai*,' explained Barney. 'We saw the video last night. Jenkinson was just demonstrating one of the karate kicks from the film.'

'Assembly, now,' ordered Mr Lanchester. 'Hop it.'

Barney, Jenks and I had been friends for years. Why, I'm not sure. You wouldn't have thought of us as kids who would end up being friends. But we were inseparable.

Barney and I were the same age, but I'd always thought of him as being older. He could be a total prat when he wanted to be, but there was always something grown-up about him. Perhaps it was because he didn't have any brothers and sisters. Perhaps his brain was a bit different from everyone else's.

He thought before he said anything, and when he said it, it always sounded right, never naff, never stupid. The way some of the teachers spoke to the rest of us, you'd think we were five-year-olds, but when they talked to Barney they sounded really matey. He didn't take any

more notice of them than we did, but they were matey nevertheless.

I suppose that's why he got away with being fat. Anyone else his size would have had the mick taken good and proper. But not Barney. You didn't tease him. Not because he'd do you in, though he might do you in if he was in the mood for doing someone in. He just seemed to be above all that sort of stuff.

Sometimes I wondered why Barney liked me. I mean, he could have picked anyone in the school to be friends with. But he'd stuck around for five years without giving me the push, so I reckoned he must have thought I was O.K.

Jenks, on the other hand, was a total prat most of the time. Sometimes he was hilarious; sometimes he was a complete wind-up. He looked like a rat, with a sharp, little nose and stiff, brown hair. He moved like a rat, too, scuttling from one place to another, hardly able to stand still for more than a second at a time. And, as Mr Lanchester once said, if his brain was dynamite, there wouldn't be enough to blow his head off. Which was an exaggeration, but not much of an exaggeration. Jenks was no Einstein.

Unlike Barney, he had so many brothers and sisters I could never remember how many there were. The Jenkinsons' house was like the chimp cage at the zoo. The two TVs were on at full blast, day and night. There was always an argument going on in the next room and someone had always just given someone else a thick ear. Which is probably why Jenks talked twice as much as a normal human being. It was what he had to do at home to get a word in edgeways. It was probably why he was so hyperactive, too – always on the move, trying to stay out of the way of the thick ears.

In short, the Crane Grove Crew were an odd mixture.

Friday was one of those long, hot, tedious school days when you know that you are going to fall asleep at the desk.

After break, we found ourselves doing the Romans in Britain with Mr Forsyth: aqueducts, straight roads, villas, the helmets with the brushes on top, etc, etc. It was going in one ear and out the other. It made *Love Hotel* seem interesting.

I felt as if someone had stitched my eyelids together with elastic. After ten minutes or so, I couldn't hold them open any longer. If I didn't do something fast, I was going to end up snoring on the desk.

As a last resort, I began pricking my finger with the point of my compass, which woke me up a treat. Now I only had to work out what to do with the blood that was oozing out of my finger. Not having a handkerchief in my pocket, I wrote Jenks' name on the desk in blood.

'Hadrian's wall runs from Wallsend-on-Tyne,' droned Mr Forsyth, rolling his map of Great Britain down over the blackboard, 'to Bowness-on-Solway. It is seventy-three miles long and has small castles every mile. At the height of the Roman Occupation, it had seventeen forts along it, each big enough for a garrison . . .' Blah, blah, blah.

It was hard to believe that Mr Forsyth was a human being. He'd only been at the school for two terms. He spoke with a snotty accent on account of his having gone to a public school, and he walked so straight it looked as if there was a plank up the back of his jacket. His trouser creases were sharp as knife blades, and he was stricter than Attila the Hun.

You could imagine other teachers going home after school finished for the day. You could imagine them having kids of their own, going out canoeing as a hobby, painting the garden shed or lounging around in the pub. But you could only ever imagine Mr Forsyth as a teacher. What he did after school, I'm not sure. Perhaps he was just put in a big box at the back of the staff room and taken out again next morning.

We didn't like him a lot.

I leant back in my chair and focused on his head. Flicking the microscopic switch concealed in my Xyrian armpit, I brought my neutron ray into action. Tiny crosswires appeared in the centre of my field of vision and I aimed these at the bridge of his glasses.

I waited for the atomic coils to warm up, then I gave the order to fire. A beam of pure, ice-blue energy shot across the classroom and vaporised Mr Forsyth where he stood, leaving only a smoking hole on the podium. I turned off the neutron ray and relaxed. The operation had gone to plan. I had not been detected.

'Ben. . . ?' he snapped.

'Yes, Mr Forsyth?' I replied, suddenly awake.

'Well. . . ?'

'Er, well what?' I was in trouble.

'Emperor Severus?' He was rolling up his sleeves. It was a bad sign, that. 'Ring any bells?'

I shook my head. 'No.'

'Have you heard a word I've said?'

It wasn't worth attempting an answer. He had stopped listening. I felt a lump in my throat. He was going to do the ruler trick. We all knew he was going to do the ruler trick. But that didn't make it any less terrifying. Silence descended on the class.

He stepped off the podium and made his way slowly down the aisle of desks towards me. He said nothing. He just let the tension thicken in the air until it was like treacle.

He stood next to me for several minutes, until I could hardly bear to wait any longer. Then he leant backwards and coiled his arm like he was going to throw a cricket ball to New Zealand. Finally he exploded. His arm became a blur and the edge of his ruler came down on the desk so hard it sounded as if a gun had gone off next to my ear.

'Detention!'

He turned smartly back to the desk and we all went limp with relief, like puppets whose strings have been cut.

'The Picts swarmed across Hadrian's Wall twice in the first hundred years after it was put up. Then Emperor Severus renovated it in 210 A.D. and kept the Picts at bay . . .'

'Don't kid me,' I said to Barney. 'I know you're Agent Z. I know you put the worms in my bed. Just admit it, O.K.?'

We were sitting at lunch. Barney was lifting the skin off his custard with the back of his spoon and trying to get it into his mouth in one piece.

'Worms?' exclaimed Barney, the skin dangling.

'You must be completely mad or something,' added Jenks.

'De-licious!' grinned Barney, swallowing.

I let the matter drop. Something was going on. Obviously, it was meant to be a secret. They'd let me in on it sooner or later. I mean, I was a fully signed-up member of the Crane Grove Crew. I had a right to know. They understood that. I cut the jammy bit out of the sponge pudding, soaked it in custard and ate it.

'Don't pig yourself,' warned Jenks. 'You don't want to get stomach cramps or indigestion or anything like that. You've got to think of your performance on the pitch this afternoon.'

'Quite,' agreed Barney, leaning down the table, taking a second pudding that a girl from 2B had left untouched and gobbling it down. 'You've got to be on top form.'

'Hup! Hup! Hup! Hup! Hup!' shouted Jenks.

He was squatting down, touching the ground and jumping into the air over and over again at the edge of the pitch, stretching his leg muscles. I'd got Kev Parks to kick the ball at me for goalie practice, and Barney was lying on the ground conserving his energy.

We were all looking forward to the match until we saw the St George's C team clamber down out of their minibus. They looked, somehow, bigger than us, wider, taller, heavier, stronger. Mind you, this was nothing new. The teams we played always looked bigger than us. Perhaps it was because we always lost. Perhaps it was because someone on our side always ended up with a gashed leg or a kicked head.

Apart from Barney, that is. He's heavier than most of the teachers. When he runs, he wobbles, and when he's dribbling the ball towards a player from the other team, you can see them thinking, 'I'll beat the fat plonker, no problem.' Then Barney runs into the player from the other team, knocks them down, runs over them and carries on running with the ball.

He does this a couple of times at the beginning of a match and terrifies the other side. After about ten minutes, however, he's shattered, and by half-time he usually persuades Mr Lanchester that he's sprained an ankle and should be substituted.

By this time, Jenks has usually been sent off. He never actually starts the fights himself. He just has a talent for irritating people. Last week, he and this player from Grimstead were going for a ball when Jenks pointed over his shoulder and screamed, 'Look out!', at the top of his voice. The player turned round and Jenks ran off with the ball. Two minutes later, the other player punched Jenks in the stomach and the game turned into a pitched battle.

Jenks keeps trying to tell Mr Lanchester that professional footballers are always getting into fights and committing fouls, but Mr Lanchester says that professional footballers are 'not good role models for young boys'.

Having said all this, we were doing rather well. The second half had started and we were winning one–nil. I had hardly touched the ball and was leaning against the posts letting them thrash St George's at the other end of the pitch.

Anyway, I had other things to think about. I'd just got a transmission from a passing Xyr fighter bomber on my built-in short-wave receiver. They had some time on their hands, so I easily persuaded them to bomb the school assembly hall for target practice.

The rest of the team, who were all human beings, couldn't see the fighter bomber, but with my ultra-sensitive eyes, I watched eagerly as the huge, silver craft circled high above the games field and directed its weapon nozzles towards the earth.

It was just as I was helping guide their lasers that I was hit on the side of the head with a football. A cheer went up.

'Goooooooooooal!'

'Brilliant,' said Jenks, walking past me into the back of the net to retrieve the ball, 'absolutely, amazingly, wonderfully brilliant.'

I stood up again. My head hurt and everything looked hazy, like a *Love Hotel* flashback.

It was in the changing room that Agent Z struck for the second time. My shoes had shrunk. That's what seemed to have happened, at any rate. I had my feet halfway in when

I realised that the shoes were at least an inch too short. Jenks and Barney were sitting opposite, so I simply put my football boots back on.

I looked more closely at the shoes. It was a classy job alright. They must have swapped them for another pair. I'd guessed that much. Even so, they'd disguised the new pair perfectly. They'd copied the scuffing on the left toe exactly; and the broken right lace, too.

I turned them over. The letter Z had been carved into the soles with a penknife. I tossed them into my gym bag and, without a backward glance, walked out of the changing room. By the time I got home, my studs were wrecked, but a plan was forming inside my head.

I had Agent Z sussed.

Mum was standing in the kitchen when I came through the door. She had her wry look on – the one where she raises an eyebrow and purses her lips. This is the look she gives me when she is about to tell me, in the nicest possible way, that I've done something totally brainless.

'Ben?' she asked.

'Yes, Mum,' I replied.

She put her rubber-gloved hand into the sink of washing and pulled out my bed sheet. Bits of it were still white; but most of it was covered in earth and squashed worm blood.

'Ben,' she repeated, 'have you got some sort of problem you're not telling me about?'

# Bad Breath and Poisoned Chocolates

On Saturday morning, I was lying in bed having this great dream about flying a biplane across the French Alps. The dream didn't last for long. I'd spun the propeller and started the engine. I'd climbed into the cockpit, buckled the strap on my leather flying cap and pulled my goggles down over my eyes. In the distance, I could see the white peaks of the mountains. I pressed the throttle and began to taxi down the runway.

Then, before I'd even got the machine off the ground, I was woken by Badger, who had pushed open my bedroom door, leapt up onto the bed and was barking into my face.

Badger is a hundred years old, or thereabouts – a half-bald Old English sheep dog. He is also completely deaf.

He leaves hair everywhere and has breath that smells of rotting brussel sprouts.

Consequently, I'm not too keen on Badger. Give me a toad any day. Toads don't need walkies. Toads don't hog the sofa. You don't get toad pooh all over your shoes when you go to the shops, and toads don't burst into your bedroom at 7a.m. and wake you up by jumping all over you.

I stood no chance whatsoever of going back to sleep with Badger's yelps ringing in my ears and his vile breath getting up my nose, so I got out of bed and did all my bathroom stuff.

Downstairs, I found Dad in the kitchen, wearing Mum's flowery apron and standing over the cooker, singing out of tune.

'Everybody in the whole cell block, uh-huh! Was dancing to the jailhouse rock, uh-huh!'

Now, there are lots of good things about Dad. He is brilliant at mending bikes, for instance, or getting my cassette player working again. He cooks an ace curry when Mum lets him (though he makes one hell of a mess), and, sometimes, he and I will wander off together on Sunday afternoons for a long walk out in the hills, or to watch a motorcycle Grand Prix, or see a film.

On the other hand, there are times when Dad acts like a spotty teenager. In particular, he can't resist singing all his favourite songs at the top of his voice, holding a spanner (or a spatula in this case) like it was a microphone. Sometimes, I come home and find he and Mum doing the Twist in the middle of the lounge. But worst of all is when he greases his hair back and puts on his leather jacket to go to the Elvis Presley Fan Club Meeting every month. All these things make me want to crawl away and hide under a stone until he becomes normal again.

'Return to sender,' he was crooning, 'dooby-doo-wah . . . Address unknown . . . shoo-bop, shoo-bop . . .'

'Dad!' I pleaded.

'What?' he asked, drumming on the edge of the frying pan with the spatula.

'The neighbours might hear.'

'The Robinsons are off on one of their nudist weekends. And the Birches never get up before eleven on a Saturday.'

He did a pelvic wiggle, then grinned. He was winding me up deliberately. 'Return to sender. . . ,' he sang.

'Bacon, egg, sausage, tomato and fried bread O.K. for Sir?'

'Sure, Dad,' I said, walking over to the open window and closing it.

After breakfast, I got the chocolates out from the back of the larder. Mad Aunt Gwen had given them to me for Christmas five months before, but they looked just about edible. I took one out and gingerly sliced the bottom off with the vegetable knife. I scooped out the Turkish Delight filling and packed the hole with Dad's favourite, extra-strong French mustard.

I heated the edges by holding them above the toaster for a few seconds until they were sticky, then pressed the two halves together again. When the chocolate had cooled down, I smoothed the join with one of Mum's nail files. It looked perfect. I did another fifteen.

In the waste paper basket, I found an old copy of *The Mirror*. I looked for the biggest letter Z in the adverts, cut it out, glued it to a card, and hid it in the second layer of chocolates.

By then, there were only fifteen minutes to go before the Crane Grove Crew Meeting. I put the chocolate box in my gym bag, and, due to the fact that I'd still not got my real shoes back, I slipped on a pair of Mum's gardening wellies, grabbed Badger's lead and hit the road.

Once inside the park, I took the path round the boating lake and went into the trees, behind the boarded-up cafe. Clambering through the undergrowth, I found my way to the gap in the fence, squeezed Badger through and walked onto the wasteground.

Behind the rusty bulldozer, I got down on all fours. From now on, I could be seen by lookouts. I had to move carefully. The yellow wellingtons were a liability, but I was stuck with them. Carefully, therefore, I crawled out from behind the big tyres and snaked my way over the rubble and the weeds to the hawthorn-covered fencing. Ripping off a branch of leaves and holding it over my fluorescent feet, I sprinted across no-man's land to the piles of bricks. Badger distracted attention by squatting to relieve himself under the far hedge.

Putting my head above the bricks, I could see the plastic Christmas-tree angel standing in the window of the Command Centre. That meant the Crew were already in residence. So, I crept round to the rear window and tapped out the rhythm of the national anthem at double speed on the cracked glass.

I waited for a minute or two, then, finally, Jenks' head slid out of the disused cat flap at the bottom of the back door. He was wearing a green, combat balaclava and his brother's swimming goggles. 'What's the password?' he demanded.

'The password?' I said.

'Yeh. You need a password. New regulations. I've just decided.'

'Jenks!' I said, getting irritated.

'You have to give me the password, I'm afraid,' he insisted. 'No password, no entry.'

'Stop being a complete wally and let me in,' I hissed, thinking I might have to punch him round the head to make him see sense.

'That'll do.' He grinned. ' "Complete wally" is the new password. I've just decided.' And with that, his head slid back inside the cat flap.

I walked round the side of the Command Centre to the cellar window. You wouldn't have known it was a cellar window. It was just below ground level, set into a brick recess. We'd nailed rubbish to an old plank and laid it over the recess. The window was invisible.

The rubbish lifted off the ground and Jenks' balaclava'd head reappeared. 'Greetings, Comrade,' he said.

'Greetings to you, too,' I replied, humouring him.

'Now get in quick,' he insisted, pulling me downwards. 'Anyone could be watching.'

I glanced behind me. Badger looked happy enough. I bent down, slipped into the recess and manoeuvred myself through the window, pulling the rubbish-board closed over my head.

Barney had discovered the Command Centre the previous summer. According to my Gran, who knows about everything that happened round here since the Romans left, it used to be the park-keeper's cottage. But there's nothing much left in Crane Grove Park these days

– just a few ducks, a roundabout and some scrubby grass with dog mess all over it. And half of it's been turned into a new housing estate. So they don't have a park-keeper anymore, just a man in a van who comes round every afternoon to pick up the litter.

The place had been boarded up by the council and the doors were chained, but Barney, Jenks and I managed to force one of the boards from the windows and get inside. It was like the Marie Celeste. There were still tables and chairs and a fridge in the kitchen. There were beds and wardrobes and bits of bric-a-brac lying around. Everything was rotted and covered in earwigs, but it was all there, even down to an old bedspread, now covered in snails. We half expected to go upstairs and find the old park-keeper's skeleton lying on the bathroom floor, as if they'd just come round one day and nailed the place up with him still inside – but we didn't.

The place was haunted, too. At least that was what Jenks told his little sister Brenda. She had overheard us talking about the Command Centre one day and wanted to come to one of our meetings. So, Jenks cooked up this story which scared her so much she never went near the park again, let alone the Command Centre.

Long before the town had been built, according to Jenks, this plot of land had been the sight of a sacrificial Druid temple where they sliced people up and drank their blood. The Druids had gone, but three spirits of the Druids' victims lived on, doomed to remain in the same place until the world ended and the earth crashed into the sun.

They were called The Beverley Sisters — three long-dead, identical girls, each dressed in rags which hid their translucent, sickly bodies. Their eyeballs were almost completely white, with only a pin-prick of black in the centre. Strangest of all, their faces were covered with blonde fur, which grew even out of their eyelids. (Jenks said Brenda started screaming and passed out when he got to this bit, but he was probably exaggerating, as usual.) They appeared at dusk and, if you were foolish enough to have stayed around too long after dark, they would seek you out and say, in high, wheezing voices, 'Come with us. Yes, come with us.'

The Beverley Sisters, decided Jenks, who was rather chuffed at having invented this story and got rather carried away with it, especially liked extra-strong mints, and the only way of protecting yourself against them was to leave a packet in the centre of the table for them to eat in the early hours of the morning. As a result, we had somehow got into the habit of taking a packet of mints along to the Command Centre at every meeting.

I jumped down onto the cellar floor and followed Jenks upstairs. Barney was sitting in the lounge on one of the mouldy chairs which we had covered with plastic sheeting. He was pouring the last scraps from a bag of chips into his mouth. 'This is for you,' he said, leaning over the arm of the chair and handing me a large, brown envelope. 'I found it on the Command Centre doorstep this morning.'

I opened the packet and took my shoes out. I kept a straight face, took off my wellingtons and put my own shoes back on. Saying nothing, I opened my gym pack, took out the chocolates to make space and shoved the wellingtons inside. I left the chocolates lying on the floor.

Jenks and Barney wanted me to say something; I could tell. They wanted me to ask them, all over again, whether they were Agent Z. But I wasn't going to give in. 'I think I need a drink,' I announced.

'Coming right up,' replied Jenks. He walked over to the fridge, which we had cleaned out, even though it didn't work. He opened it, took out a can of Coke and threw it. 'Catch!'

'Cheers!' I tugged the ring-pull off. 'How's things?'

'Got a detention yesterday,' he complained.

'Snap,' I answered.

'. . . for writing my name in blood on one of the desks in Forsyth's room.'

'Really?' I replied, pulling my shirtsleeve down over my scabby fingertip.

'Strange, isn't it,' he mused.

'Very strange,' I replied.

We'd turned the lounge into the main bunker of the Command Centre. We'd cut a hole in the planking over the window, and, with the help of the binoculars Barney had got for his last birthday, we could look out through the trees and watch what went on in the park, and in the windows of the houses on the estate. Inside, we'd stuck motorbike posters over one of the walls and silver foil all over another.

The facing wall, however, looked oddly like a map of the countryside. It was covered in a green and brown leaf-pattern wallpaper, which was now covered with patches of moss and damp and fungus. Not wanting to waste this, Jenks had brought along all the toy soldiers, tanks and armoured cars which he was now too grown up to play with, and glued them, feet- wheels- and tracks-first, onto the wallpaper.

The whole wall now looked like a vast battlefield running from the skirting board to the ceiling. It would have been more realistic if it had been on the floor, but then we'd just have trodden all over it. Besides, if you turned your head on its side, it looked just as good.

Over the months, we'd added roads made out of black electrical tape, rivers made of Cellophane, and bridges made out of cardboard. We'd tried to make trees out of branches from the park, but we still hadn't worked out how to make branches stick on to the wall. Barney was going to borrow his Dad's drill to make holes we could jam them into, but we had to wait till his parents went away for the weekend to do that.

It didn't matter. It looked realistic enough without trees. You could sit facing it and imagine you were a fighter pilot coming in over enemy country, your finger on the missile-release trigger, ready to take out the airfield. We had a potato gun in the fridge that you could use to make it more realistic, and sometimes you could knock a tank off the wall if you were accurate. But you had to be careful. Some time ago, Jenks had used his catapult, blown up a bridge and brought an entire roll of wallpaper down, tanks, men, rivers and all. It took us two whole weekends to glue it up again.

It was about ten minutes later that Barney was sick. With the chips gone, I knew that it was only a matter of time, and, sure enough, he couldn't resist. I soon saw his hands wandering closer and closer to the chocolates. The lid was slipped quietly off and the chocolates started coming out of the box, one by one, and into his mouth.

'Provisions,' he nodded to me, when he saw that he'd been spotted. 'An army marches on its stomach.'

I let him carry on.

His luck was in at first. Nougat, caramel, fudge, praline; he was somehow managing to pick all the undoctored ones from the top layer.

Then I hit jackpot. Unable to resist any longer, he stuffed two into his mouth at once, a strawberry delight and a Ben's Special Mustard Surprise. He crunched them between his teeth like a hungry camel.

Jenks and I were in the middle of talking about his brother's Kawasaki. Suddenly, Barney sat bolt upright and began making one of the strangest sounds I had ever heard: a sort of gurgling, strangling, screaming, choking noise. He went pop-eyed and an unpleasant chocolate-brown gunge started oozing out from between his lips. He looked like something from *The Exorcist*. He struggled to his feet and stumbled blindly towards the bathroom.

'What's up with him?' Jenks asked.

I shrugged my shoulders. Jenks walked over to the chocolates and began investigating them as if they were an unexploded bomb. Eventually, he lifted the top layer and picked out the big Z.

As Barney retched helplessly next door, Jenks laughed and turned towards me. 'I get it,' he said. 'What a laugh. Good job *I'm* not a gut bucket, isn't it?'

When Barney had finally finished vomiting, he came back through to the main bunker and saw the Z that Jenks had left lying on top of the chocolate box. He narrowed his eyes at me, then decided it would be unsporting to get cross. After the worms and the shoes and everything. Instead, he began to smile slyly and washed his mouth out with the rest of my Coke. 'Welcome to the club,' he announced, shaking my hand. 'I think Agent Z will be glad to have you on board.'

'Great,' I agreed.

That done, Barney carefully cut all the remaining chocolates in half to find out which he could carry on eating. Then we did all the initiation stuff. I got the badge. I was then told the code words. I learnt the secret sign. Jenks wanted to cut a Z-shape into my forearm with Barney's penknife, like they'd done in *Return of the Killer Samurai*, but we settled for writing it in biro.

And I was in.

# Uh-Oh!

I was a bit preoccupied on Monday morning, for two reasons. Firstly, I'd got a bit of flak over breakfast on account of the wellington boots. It wasn't until Mum was jamming her toast that she got round to asking, 'Ben, you haven't seen my wellingtons anywhere have you?'

Which is when I suddenly remembered that I'd borrowed them to go to the Command Centre on Saturday morning. Feeling guilty, I picked my gym bag off the floor, took them out and gave them back.

'I had to do the gardening in your football boots,' she added, 'seeing as there wasn't anything else to wear. It's a jolly good job you've got feet like flippers.'

'Sorry, Mum,' I apologised, returning the stolen property. 'Give you good grip, though, football boots.'

'Grip is irrelevant,' she replied a bit sharply. 'I was trimming the rhododendrons, Ben, not playing wing threequarter for Tottenham Hotspur.'

'Wing threequarter is rugby, not football,' I corrected her.

'He's right, I'm afraid,' confirmed Dad through a mouthful of cornflakes.

'I don't know,' Mum groaned, wagging her butter knife at both of us. 'You two! You are enough to send a grown woman insane.'

Mind you, Mum had her reasons for being a bit off that morning. The night before, things hadn't gone too well in the Sunday edition of *Love Hotel*. Brad Piston was driving to a secluded beach villa in his Maserati to meet Lucinda Diamond, the wealthy heiress he'd fallen idiotically in love with. What he didn't know was that Ernie had cut the brake cables. To cut a long and tedious story short, the car went haywire on a twisty mountain road and before you could say, 'Good riddance', the Maserati had broken through the crash barriers and was plunging downwards through the air into a rocky gorge.

Which seemed like a pretty good thing to me, Brad Piston being a major slimeball, but Mum had the hots for him. He was 'handsome and masterful', so she said. Which made me wonder why on earth she fell in love with Dad. But, then, they can both be a bit of a mystery at times.

The second reason I was feeling a bit preoccupied was the worrying fact that Presley was still off the cat food. I guessed he might just be bored of Tuna and Pilchard, so

I'd persuaded Mum to buy Rabbit and Heart instead. But it made no difference. He was on hunger strike, make no mistake. He didn't even taste it.

I wondered whether the vet would be able to do anything. I trusted Mr Anderson. He'd already told Mum, three times, that Badger ought to be put down for his own good, being so old and having bad arthritis. And anyone who suggested putting Badger down had their head screwed on right.

On the other hand, however, I couldn't imagine Dr Anderson pulling out all the stops to keep Presley alive. I mean, he was only a toad, and nobody goes gooey over toads, not like they do over cats and dolphins and donkeys and old dogs with arthritis and bad breath. Even Mr Anderson would probably just say it was cruel to let him live any longer, stuff a needle in his bum and chuck him in the wastebin.

On the way to school, I was imagining a toad on an operating table, being saved from certain death by heroic doctors in green masks and overalls, when I bumped into Miss Phelps again. 'Hello Ben,' she said. 'I told Geoffrey about the spark plugs, but he gave me a funny look and said there wasn't anything wrong with the car. Thanks for being so considerate, though.'

On account of thinking about Presley undergoing surgery, it took me a few minutes to remember that I had been a hyper-being from the Xyr Galaxy with ultrasonic hearing on Friday morning. I suddenly felt guilty about having fed her all that guff about the spark plugs. Still, it was too late to come clean, now. If I owned up, she'd have thought I'd gone completely insane. 'Any time,' I said, and hoped she'd forget about it.

We did a few verses of *There Is A Green Hill Far Away* in assembly, then listened to some girl in the fifth form giving a talk about raising money for Africa.

After assembly, we were tortured with maths for forty-five minutes. X plus Q minus S divided by a few thousands multiplied by any telephone number you can think of etc, etc. It would have given Sherlock Holmes a brain haemorrhage. Still, as Mum said, I had a fertile imagination, and I'd probably end up being an artist. And artists didn't have to add up.

At break, Agent Z went into operation.

Jenks and I met up with Barney at the corner of the entrance hall. He pretended not to notice us at first, then threw a glance around the room before turning over his lapel and showing us his Z badge. We did the same.

'Eady-ray?' he asked.

'Eady-ray,' we replied.

'Ave-hay ou-yay ot-gay e-thay equipment-way?'

'Es-yay,' Jenks confirmed. He lifted the corner of his satchel to reveal the end of a roll of clingfilm and pulled the corner of a boot polish tin from his jacket pocket.

'Ight-ray . . . ynchronise-say atches-way.'

We rolled our cuffs back and synchronised our watches.

'O-way. A-kay,' said Barney. 'Enks-jay, ou-yay over-cay or-fay us-way. En-bay, ets-lay o-gay in-way and-way it-hay e-thay oilets-tay.'

'O-way. A-kay.' I gave him the thumbs-up.

We slipped stealthily into the toilets. A couple of boys were standing at the urinals, and two fifth formers were beating each other up in the corner. They were probably not going to be artists when they grew up. We waited until they had finished and then went into action.

Jenks walked casually over to the sink and began washing his hands, keeping his ears cocked and his eyes peeled. Meanwhile, Barney and I went into two adjacent cubicles – me with the clingfilm, him with the boot polish, swapping them beneath the partition when we had finished.

The clingfilm we smoothed down over the toilet bowls, pulling it tight until it was invisible. The boot polish we spread in a thin layer over the black, plastic toilet seats, patting it down with paper so that it blended perfectly. We then put stickers on the back of each cubicle door reading; 'WITH LOVE FROM AGENT Z.'

'One-day?' asked Barney.

'One-day,' I replied.

'Ets-lay it-splay!'

We came out of the cubicles and gave microscopic nods to Jenks. He slipped away. Barney and I then moved over to the sinks and soaped the incriminating polish stains

41

off our hands. As planned, I towelled my hands dry first and walked surreptitiously towards the doors.

As I turned the corner, however, I walked straight onto the toes of Fisty Morgan's shoes. This was a hiccup we had not expected.

Fisty Morgan was a psychopath, two years above us. He had something wrong inside his head – like they'd taken his real brain out and put a gorilla's brain in its place. At the beginning of the summer term he'd been suspended for getting into a fight with Mr Lanchester. Mr Lanchester, who is six foot three, had got the upper hand eventually, but it was a close run thing.

Fisty used to threaten some of the smaller kids and make them hand over their pocket money. He'd done the same to Jenks the previous week – demanded five quid

protection money in return for not beating Jenks up. At the time, Jenks had just looked over Fisty's shoulder, said, 'Hello Sir', then scarpered while Fisty turned round. Fisty had threatened to break Jenks' arm for that, sometime.

Fisty told everyone that his Dad was in prison for armed robbery, and he was going to go into the same line of business after he left school. We all believed him. After all, we couldn't imagine anyone giving him a real job. Bank robbery seemed right up his street.

'Orry-say,' I said, stepping back off his shoes.

'What?' he barked.

'S-s-sorry, I mean,' I stammered.

I noticed, out of the corner of my eye that Barney had left by the other door. This was what we had agreed over the weekend. If one of us fell into enemy hands, we had to split up. If we were tortured, we had sworn, on our graves, not to give the others' names away. It was all part of the Agent Z Code.

'Sorry,' I repeated. My voice had gone all squeaky. I sounded like a complete berk, but I was too frightened to worry about the impression I was making.

Fisty stepped forward until I was forced back against the wall. He pushed the tip of his index finger into my adam's apple and grunted, 'You will be.'

He pushed past me and several small kids at the urinals ran away. I walked out into the corridor as he went into one of the cubicles and shut the door behind him. I turned slowly towards the entrance hall again and began to run. Barney and Jenks were waiting for me. I was hardly past the secretary's office, when I heard a blood-curdling scream from behind me. Barney winced. I winced.

'Whassat?' asked Jenks, jumping nervously, and looking around him.

I pointed behind me.

Down the corridor, Fisty stormed out of the toilets, his grey trousers splashed with dark, wet patches.

'Morgan!' Mr Lanchester shouted, bringing Fisty to a halt in the middle of the corridor. 'Would you care to explain yourself?'

The school day seemed to go on for ever. We were terrified that, at any moment, Fisty Morgan would work out who had clingfilmed the toilets, burst into the room where we were sitting and beat us to a pulp.

On top of which, Jenks and I had detention to look forward to. When the bell went, we watched everyone else disappear through the school gates. Then Jenks and I made our way to room F17 to receive our punishment. We'd catch up with Barney later.

Under the gaze of Potato-Head Dawson, some twenty of us made our way to our allotted desks. He glanced down his typed sheet and read out the work teachers had ordered their pupils to do over the coming hour: redoing sums, drawing maps of Asia, writing essays on King Henry the Eighth, that sort of thing.

We, however, were Mr Forsyth's detainees. Being old-fashioned, he'd given us lines – 1,000 of them. 'Hadrian's Wall was built in 122 A.D.' for me, and 'I must not write my name on the desk' for Jenks.

Punishments assigned, Potato-Head sat down at the front of the room, opened his briefcase, took out a scruffy sheaf of paper and started reading.

He had been known as Potato-Head ever since he arrived at the school to teach art. Not because we disliked him. Actually, he was an alright sort of bloke. He liked an easy life and he was a bit of a pushover when it came to homework and so on. Added to which, he seemed to get into trouble with the rest of the staff almost as much as we did – for skiving off to the pub at lunchtime, or smoking behind the sports equipment shed while on break duty. That type of thing.

As for his nickname, he got it for the simple reason that he really did look just like a potato – fat and lumpy with the odd, huge spot here and there.

If the truth be told, Potato-Head didn't have to pretend he was working behind his briefcase. We all knew he was reading a sci-fi paperback like he usually did. It didn't bother us. We'd have been doing the same thing in his position.

I had my 1,000 lines done in fifteen minutes. This was possible on account of the line-writing machine that Dad had shown me how to make: ten biros Sellotaped in a row between two rulers. Apparently, he used to use one when he was at school several hundred years ago when Elvis was king. An old idea, but it worked a treat.

Consequently, when the mysterious flying object came through the window, I was already sitting back and looking up at the blackboard wondering what I was going to have for tea. It sped in from the right-hand side of the classroom, rose in a high arc under the strip lights and bounced on Potato-Head's desk. Lazily, he slipped the

45

novel back into the briefcase, stood up and retrieved the object from the corner of the room, turning it in his hands.

I could see then what it was – a large, scrubbed potato with the letter Z carved into the surface.

'Very strange,' he said casually to the rest of us. Then he turned and hurled it back out of the same window it had come from. Only when he sat down did we hear the sound of glass breaking from the car park two storeys down.

He sighed and shook his head. 'Ben?' he called out to me at the back.

'Yes Sir?'

'Go and shut the window will you? And don't let anyone see you doing it, O.K.?'

## Orang-utans and Killer Crabs

The three of us were at the Command Centre the following evening.

Barney didn't seem to be bothered about Fisty Morgan. True, Barney was bigger than Fisty, but Fisty could probably have floored a rhinoceros with one punch. Still, Barney had said, 'Worrying about it doesn't help' and that was that. No worries.

Jenks and I, on the other hand, were petrified. Jenks was pacing round and round like a crazed animal, muttering constantly. 'He's going to find out . . . He'll realise it was us . . . He's going to get us . . . We're going to be dead . . . There's nothing we can do . . .'

As usual, I was miles away. It seemed like the best solution. I was standing at the window, focusing Barney's binoculars on a woman in a raincoat standing at the edge of the pond. She had been feeding the ducks from her bag of breadcrumbs for some minutes, and now she was turning back towards the old café. As she did so, she pulled something from her pocket and dropped it into one of the litter bins. It had to be the microfilm.

I recognised her face from the slides we had been shown by the CIA man at the briefing in New York. She had the same narrow eyes, the same cheekbones, the same straight, black hair. It was definitely her – the infamous Xiao-Xiao Ptoing.

She had thrown the javelin for China in the 1976 Olympics. She had a black belt in karate. She had been trained to fly fighter aircraft. But, most important of all, she was an undercover agent for the Chinese secret service.

The microfilm she had thrown into the bin contained the blueprints for the Kennedy Space City. The Space City was a top secret American project that virtually no-one knew about. It had been built underground in the Nevada Desert and, next month, was going to be blasted into orbit – a huge, revolving structure of glass and metal where thousands of people were going to live, high above the atmosphere. The Chinese wanted the plans. They didn't like the idea of thousands of waffle-eating, Mickey-mouse-T-shirt-wearing Americans zooming through the sky high above Beijing. They were going to sabotage the project.

I swivelled the binoculars back and forth. Sooner or later, her contact would arrive to retrieve the microfilm and get it shipped back to Nanjing. Was it the man with the beard and the walking boots and the pushchair on the far side of the pond? Or had the Chinese secret service shrunk someone with special scientific techniques and disguised them as the toddler who was pushing the plastic boat out onto the water? Maybe the Alsatian was really a robot controlled by someone hiding nearby.

I swivelled the binoculars back again and saw that Xiao-Xiao Ptoing was now sitting on a park bench, casually reading a newspaper. It was crafty that. A less professional spy would just have walked off. That would have been a dead giveaway.

Suddenly, the binoculars were taken out of my hands by Barney. Chewing the remains of a biscuit, he pressed the lenses to his eyes and peered out through the porthole. 'Could be wrong there, Ben,' he said. 'That's Mrs Abrahams. She works at the off-licence down by the garage.'

'Oh,' I said, coming down to earth.

I walked back to the centre of the room and reached out to take one of the Beverley Sisters' mints. Normally, this would have been O.K. I mean, we knew that they didn't actually come and eat them in the night, and it would be a waste just to leave them there. But today, I had a nervous feeling in the pit of my stomach. I left them alone.

'He must have known it was us. He *must* have known,' muttered Jenks, collapsing onto the sofa and springing up again immediately. 'He's stupid. I *know* he's stupid. But he's not *that* stupid. Is he? What I mean is . . .'

'Put a sock in it, Jenks,' I snapped. I was worried enough already, without Jenks ramming the point home.

'Put a sock in it? Put a sock in it?' Jenks shouted back, waving his arms around like a windmill. 'We're all going to get our arms broken, and all you can say is "Put a sock in it"?' He leant against the wall, panting heavily, 'I feel sick.'

'Well, go and be sick,' I said. 'Somewhere else.'

'Thanks a lot, Ben,' he replied sarcastically. 'You're being a really good friend, I don't think. You're lucky. I already owe him five quid. He's already threatened to do me in for that. Just you wait. You wait till those big fists start mashing your face up. Then you'll know why I'm scared.'

I didn't need reminding about this. For a day now, I had been able to feel the pressure of Fisty's finger pressed into my adam's apple. Jenks was not helping.

I was on the verge of mashing Jenks' own face up a bit, just to keep him quiet, when Barney reappeared from the cellar. 'I think you're overestimating our man,' he announced. He was carrying a large sheet of card we hadn't seen before. 'Agent Z is swift, silent and invisible,' he added. 'Fisty Morgan is thick as two short planks.' He walked over to the Crew notice board and pinned up the sheet of card. On it was a large photocopied picture of Fisty Morgan's head attached to the body of an orang-utan.

'Brilliant!' I said.

It *was* brilliant, too.

It was even making Jenks smile. 'Where d'you get *that*?' asked Jenks.

'I got ape-brain's picture from the athletics team photo,'

explained Barney, 'and the orang-utan's from the school library. The rest I did with the photocopier at Dad's office. Good, isn't it?'

'Wicked,' I said, and began to laugh.

Barney stood back from the picture, walked over to the fridge and took out a can of Coke. He returned to the picture, shook the can, opened it and squirted a large Z of fizz all over Fisty's monkey legs.

It was getting dark, so we took the plastic Christmas tree angel out of the window, bolted the door of the main bunker, went into the cellar and climbed up onto the ground. Badger was waiting by the bulldozer, catching a quick nap before I forced him to walk home again.

'Tomorrow, then,' I said.

'Roger,' said Barney.

'Roger who?' asked Jenks.

'Lord preserve us!' moaned Barney.

'*Ciao*,' I said, clipping Badger's lead onto his collar.

We did the Z sign in the air and went off in three different directions so that we couldn't be followed by the KGB.

I was feeling pretty buoyed up until Badger and I got to Fairfield Road. Barney's picture had put things in perspective. He was right. Fisty couldn't put two and two together, except to make five and a half. He'd never twig.

But the sight of Fisty himself standing at the bus shelter with some mates put things in a different perspective altogether. He was sitting on a moped, chatting up Sharon Mortimer who was wearing high heels and lipstick. He was revving the throttle and trying to look like he was twenty-eight. He was succeeding, too.

I nearly wet myself. Giddy with fear, I leant back against the wall to stop myself falling over. Like Jenks said, I could just feel those big, knuckly fists raining down onto my face. I could see Mum and Dad weeping over a little Ben-sized coffin.

According to the strict codes of Agent Z undercover operations, of course, I should have just walked past. Rule 17 says, 'Keep cool.' And Barney was right. Fisty probably didn't realise that the toilets had anything to do with us. There was absolutely nothing to be afraid of. But even Agent Z has his off days. I was absolutely petrified.

I hung back and came to a standstill behind a post box. Badger was glad of the rest and lay down. There was another way round, but it meant cutting back through the park and going under the railway bridge. It would take at least ten minutes and in ten minutes there would be one cold supper and a black mark for Ben.

Which is when I saw the Phelps' Fiesta turn into the road. Mrs Phelps took the Ecology Club after school on Tuesday evenings. Mr Phelps must have just picked her up. Thinking with lightning speed, I grabbed my knee with one hand, stumbled a bit and waved at them with the other hand.

Agent Z Emergency Plan No. 348 ran without a hitch. They pulled immediately over to the kerb and Mrs Phelps wound down the window. 'Are you alright, Ben?'

'No, not really,' I groaned in mock agony.

'What's the matter?' she asked.

'I've got these sort of shooting pains in my leg,' I said, twitching a bit for effect. 'This is very rude of me, but could you give me a lift? I only live round the corner.'

'Of course we can, can't we Geoffrey?'

Mr Phelps nodded and I hauled myself onto the back seat. Badger climbed in beside me and I crossed my fingers, hoping he'd peed enough for one evening.

'Ben, this is my husband Geoffrey,' smiled Mrs Phelps, 'Geoffrey, this is Ben.'

We pulled away from the kerb and drove smoothly past Fisty Morgan.

'Ah, so you're the lad who knows so much about cars?' grinned Mr Phelps looking over his shoulder. 'One of my spark plugs wasn't firing properly, eh?' He chuckled and winked at me. He'd got me sussed alright. I felt like a complete and total wally. At least he wasn't giving the game away to Mrs Phelps. I was glad about that.

'Now, do you need some help to the door?' asked Mrs Phelps as we drew up outside the house.

'I'll be fine,' I said. 'Really.'

'And you promise you'll get your mum to take you to see the doctor?'

'Promise,' I agreed, hobbling up the path, 'and thanks very much for the lift.'

It was gone supper time and we were sitting in the lounge. Barney's picture had calmed me down a bit, but, after having seen Fisty at the bus stop, horrible thoughts had begun to lurk in the back of my mind, forcing me to give up on the maths homework.

Mum was stretched out on the sofa knitting a vile pink cardigan for Mad Aunt Gwen's baby daughter and reading Lesson 5 from *Teach Yourself Turkish* (on account of Dad having got a bit adventurous and just booked this cheap summer holiday in Fetiyeh).

'Ehliyet imtihani diye bir şey yok Belçika'da,' she said. 'Knit one. Pearl two.'

Dad was taking a carburettor apart on the dining table and I was watching *The Invasion of the Killer Crabs* in black and white. They'd just crawled up out of the freezing surf onto the pebbled beaches and started making their way towards the village. Old Perkins, the lighthouse keeper, knew something was up when he was

woken by the clicking of thousands of big, bony claws in the night. He decides to go outside and investigate, which was unbelievably stupid, but fairly predictable for this kind of film. He puts on his sou'wester and steps out into a fog so thick you couldn't see ten centimetres in front of your face and, suddenly, chomp! his legs are gobbled by a crustacean the size of a delivery van.

Which would have been a real gas under normal circumstances. This evening, however, I couldn't stop thinking that my own legs might get crunched by an orang-utan the size of a delivery van by the end of the week. I picked up the remote control and changed to a programme about folk dancing in the Ukraine.

'Dad?' I said, 'Were you ever bullied at school?'

'Nope,' he said casually. 'I was never bullied, Ben.'

'Oh,' I replied.

'Why do you ask?'

'I just wondered.'

I guessed that that was going to be the end of the conversation. I'd really wanted Mum or Dad to say, 'Why? Is someone bullying you?' I could have told them about Fisty then. I could have got everything off my chest. But, for some reason, I just couldn't say it out of the blue. They had to ask first. And then I realised that it wasn't going to be the end of the conversation. Dad had suddenly gone all serious and thoughtful.

'Do you know why I was never bullied, Ben?' he asked.

I began to cringe.

He put his screwdriver down on the table, sat back and rubbed his forehead with his hand. 'I wasn't bullied, Ben, because it was *me* who did all the bullying round our way.'

I hit the volume knob. A weird silence fell on the room. Mum put down her book and stopped knitting. I turned round towards the table. Behind me the twizzling Ukrainians carried on twizzling as if nothing had happened.

'Wow!' I said. I didn't know whether to be amazed or ashamed.

'I was a bit of a handful, I was,' Dad explained. 'A right little tearaway. Used to hang around with some real bad lads.' He looked at the ceiling as if searching for spiders. 'No, that's not right. Some real bad lads used to hang around me.'

'You never told me,' I said.

Actually, Dad had told me quite a bit about his childhood, but it used to bore me silly. So, whenever he started reminiscing, I always invented something else I had to go and do straight away.

'Come off it, Ben,' he said, half smiling. 'What do you think I should have said? "By the way, Ben, your old Dad used to beat up other kids at school, and nick cars, and go into town on a Saturday night to get smashed and punch a few skinheads"? Eh? Besides, it's not something I'm particularly proud of.'

'So, you had skinheads, even then?'

'Oh yes, Ben, and radios, and electricity, and the wheel.' He hit me playfully over the head with a magazine. 'I'm being serious.'

'He was quite a nasty piece of work,' added Mum.

I was flabbergasted. Dad had always seemed so quiet. He didn't drink. He didn't smoke. He just listened to Elvis records and messed about with the car. I couldn't imagine him punching someone.

'Why?' I said. 'Why did you beat people up?'

Dad shrugged his shoulders and stared into the distance. I didn't feel embarrassed anymore. I was just fascinated. It was like watching an in-depth TV documentary about your own parents.

'That's a difficult question, that one,' he said, quietly.

'Come on,' Mum said. 'You know why you did it. You've told me about it before now. Tell Ben.'

Dad rubbed his forehead a bit more, then finally said, 'I suppose . . . I suppose it was because I was a bit of a failure, really. I was a bonehead at school, and I was always in trouble at home. I failed every exam I ever took, and, to put the tin lid on it, none of the other kids liked me very much.'

'Oh,' I said.

It was difficult to imagine people not liking Dad. Sure, when he was in his Elvis jacket he was a prize plonker, and I used to pray that none of my teachers would recognise him in the street, but I wouldn't have changed him for anything. He could have done ballroom dancing as a hobby and I'd have chosen him over all the fathers I knew – probably.

'You see,' he carried on, 'I reckoned that if I couldn't make people like me, I could make them scared of me instead. And if I couldn't be good at school work, then I could at least be tough . . .'

57

'But . . .' I interrupted.

'Yes, I know, Ben,' he nodded. 'It was a pretty stupid reason.'

Another silence fell on the room. The Ukrainians twizzled on. It was odd, but I suddenly felt really proud of Dad. He was telling me that he used to be a bully. He was telling me that he used to be stupid. But that only made him seem wiser, more grown-up, more sussed-out. And I was flattered, too, that he was telling me these things. He trusted me.

I'd wanted to tell him about Fisty, and how I might get beaten up if I wasn't very lucky. It didn't seem so important now. It had all made Fisty seem a bit pathetic.

Finally, I said, 'So, what happened, then?'

'What do you mean?' asked Dad.

'How come you turned out . . . sort of alright.'

'Sort of alright!' chuckled Mum. 'Now there's a compliment to your father.'

'It was your mum's doing,' said Dad, who wasn't chuckling. 'She set me on the straight and narrow.'

'That I did,' Mum added.

'I met her down at The Roadmenders. It's an old pub they pulled down years back to make way for that DIY megastore,' he continued, getting stuck into the carburettor again. 'Anyway, they used to have live bands there on Fridays and Saturdays. We used to go down there and get deafened, sink a few beers and usually end up having a punch-up on the derelict land out the back with whoever we could wind up. Skinheads usually. Well, that's where I met your mum. Her brother was in this blues band that played there regularly. She and her mates used to tag along. She was a real little mover in those days,' he grinned.

Mum scowled at him jokingly.

'As she still is, of course,' he corrected himself.

I began to get that slightly queasy feeling I used to get whenever I found Mum and Dad cuddling on the sofa in front of a movie.

'Well,' continued Dad, 'it was love at first sight. We started going out together and, pretty soon, she gave me an ultimatum. Either I started behaving, or she'd chuck me. So that was it, really. I had to make up my mind. It was either marrying your mum, or ending up behind bars sooner or later.'

'It's all true,' said Mum. 'Every word.'

Silence fell on the room again. Mum reopened her book and picked up her knitting needles again. Dad put the carburettor to one side and started wiping his oily hands. I turned round and changed channels in time to see the village postmaster firing a shotgun at a killer crab at point blank range. The shot bounced off the crab's shell. It stood still for a few seconds and waggled its eyes-on-sticks at the postmaster before snapping his shotgun in half with its pincers. The postmaster screamed and they cut to a dog-biscuit commercial.

'Salonun duvarlarini boyatacaktim,' said Mum very carefully, lingering over the words.

'Dad?' I asked.

'What, Ben?' he replied.

'Were you handsome and masterful in those days?'

'Pardon?' said Dad, giving me a bog-eyed look.

Mum, who knew exactly what I was on about, laughed out loud, then narrowed her eyes at me. 'You be careful, you cheeky monster.'

That night I had the weirdest dream I'd ever had in my entire life. It all happened in the DIY megastore, I think. Elvis Presley was playing on a stage down at the far end near the bathroom section and there were crowds of people dancing to the music.

But the people were all mixed up and confused, like they are in dreams. Fisty Morgan was there, riding around on this moped in huge, lace-up army boots, with all his hair shaved off, skinhead-style. Except that he wasn't Fisty Morgan. He was my dad, and Sharon Mortimer was my mum.

Up on the stage, Mr Forsyth was playing bass guitar in Elvis Presley's backing band. He had a ripped leather jacket, stubble, long, greasy hair and tiny, round sunglasses.

I was only a baby in the dream and I was in a pushchair at the side of the dance floor. Mrs Phelps was kneeling down next to me, saying, 'He's going to be an artist when he grows up. He's got a fertile imagination.' Mr Phelps was saying, 'Well, he's certainly not going to be a car mechanic, that's for sure.'

# Fab

I kept bumping into Mrs Phelps on the way to school. Worse, every time I bumped into her, I went and gave her yet another stupid story. I couldn't help it. I did it again the following week.

'Hello, Ben,' she smiled, 'how's the leg?'

'Uh?' I replied. I hadn't got a clue what she was on about.

'Your leg,' she insisted. 'Geoffrey and I gave you a lift last . . .'

'Oh yes,' I remembered. 'It, er, got better.'

'You went to the doctor, then?'

'Yes, Mum took me a couple of days ago.'

'I hope it wasn't anything serious?'

'Well . . .' I had to think fast. 'Not *incredibly* serious.'

'It looked pretty bad to me.'

'It comes and goes, you know.'

'How awful.'

'He says I'll probably have the attacks, on and off, for the rest of my life.' I was getting carried away. There was no stopping me.

'That's terrible,' she said, looking extremely worried.

'If I'm really unlucky,' I continued, getting into my stride now, 'and it gets really bad, it might have to come off.'

'Amputated?' She went white and I wondered, momentarily, whether she was going to pass out.

'Amputated,' I agreed.

'Goodness me!' Her eyes had doubled in size and she was shaking her head. 'I must say that you're bearing up very well in the circumstances.'

I nodded my head slowly. 'Anyway, thanks for asking. I must be off.'

I turned and ran into the entrance hall.

As assembly drew to an end, Mr Lanchester pounded out the final chord of the hymn on the electric organ, we all sat down again and Sharon Mortimer walked up to the lectern. She recited a poem by William Blake about a chimney sweep and then read this piece that her class had put together. It was all about being God's children and purity and innocence and that sort of thing. Which was a bit steep, really, when we all knew that you could find her behind the gym block every lunch time, smoking cigarettes and snogging Fisty Morgan.

But Mrs Block, the headmistress, didn't know anything about what went on behind the gym block at lunch times, so she just sat back and closed her eyes and gave everyone that dreamy, holy smile she had on her face when she read the sad bits from the Bible in R.E. – when someone's been raised from the dead, or turned into a pillar of salt or a burning bush.

After Sharon Mortimer had done her bit and returned to her place, Breezeblock kept her eyes closed for a couple of minutes, so we could all meditate on being pure and innocent. Then she stood up. 'It is a bit ironic,' she said, swapping the smile for a grimace, 'that I should have to follow that moving reading with something far less pleasant. Last week, I was driving out of the school car park after a parent-teacher meeting when a *po-ta-to* came through my window. And it is not funny, Jenkinson!'

She jabbed her finger towards the back of the hall where Jenks was trying to suppress a giggle and failing miserably. 'I am not completely blind . . .' A hush fell on the school. 'This little prank was both dangerous and foolish – the act of someone with a very small mind.'

I looked behind her. Mr Dawson was pretending to scrape a stain off his tie, bending his head down to hide his crimson cheeks. It was brilliant.

'I have little doubt that this act of childish vandalism is not unconnected to a series of practical jokes with which the school has been plagued over the past weeks. Now, *you* may think these are funny. Well, when I find out who is responsible, you – whoever you are – will be laughing on the other side of your faces, because I am going to come down on you like a ton of bricks . . .'

What Breezeblock was saying, in short, was that Agent Z had managed to liven up a long, hot, boring summer term. No-one had come to any harm. Some people had got boot polish on their bums, but nothing more serious than that. As for the potato, it was entirely Mr Dawson's fault, and nothing to do with our undercover operations.

We had followed up the raid on the toilets by putting papier-mâché in a selection of the gym shoes in the changing rooms. Hanging next to the radiator, they hardened nicely over lunch. Even the fact that the idiot Jenks had accidentally filled my own shoes with papier-mâché didn't dampen our amusement at watching boys leaping into their sports gear in the afternoon, standing up, squawking in pain, then falling over.

On Wednesday morning, we had Mrs Phelps for Science. She came in, exactly as planned, carrying the large, brown parcel addressed to her, which had been left by Agent Z at the secretary's office. She put it on her desk and began opening it, talking at the same time. 'As you will remember, we were talking, last Wednesday, about atoms, the tiny particles out of which everything around us is made . . .'

Under the first layer of brown paper was a large

cardboard box. She cut away the Sellotape from the box, opened it and found another parcel inside. Undeterred, she soldiered on. 'You will also remember that there are many different types of atom, and that substances which are made up of only one kind of atom are called elements. Can anyone remember the names of some of those elements?'

'Oxygen, Mrs Phelps,' said a girl at the back.

'Carbon,' said Barney.

'Air, Mrs . . .' said Robert Chiltern.

'Not air, Robert,' Mrs Phelps frowned. 'Air is made up of several elements. Oxygen and. . . ?'

She was frowning partly because she had now un-wrapped six, successive layers of cardboard and paper and Sellotape. Finally, she gave up asking us questions altogether and gave all her attention to the mystery parcel. Within five minutes, she had unwrapped all thirty-three layers. Inside the matchbox, she found tissue paper, and in the tissue paper a folded square of paper. She opened it and out fell a tiny label attached to a piece of cotton with a knot on the end. In miniature writing on the label were the words:

'AN ATOM'

We covered the bust of the school's founder in wrapping paper. We put a mousetrap inside Henry Oliver's underwear while he was playing football. We sneaked into the school kitchen one lunch time and poured a bumper pack of black, plastic tarantulas into the gravy.

No-one suspected a thing. They had no reason to. Agent Z was fiendish, swift and undetectable. The only clues to the nature of his operations were the Z stickers at the scene of each attack – those and the notice board in the Command Centre. Here, we kept a meticulous record of each mission.

We wrote out careful descriptions of these and pinned them to the wall, along with any trophies we had collected (the under-sized shoes, the 'ATOM' label taken from Mrs Phelps' bin, a plastic tarantula and so on) and we gave each mission marks out of ten for Daring, Success and Laugh Value.

Perhaps this was why I had stopped daydreaming quite so much. Life was just too much fun.

Apart from stringing Mrs Phelps along about my leg (which was an accident that had got rather out of control), I was on planet earth virtually all the time. And why not? Planet earth was a hoot. Added to which, Agent Z's missions were complex and dangerous, and needed careful planning and intense concentration.

Dad seemed pleased by the change that had come over me. 'Nice to have you with us so much of the time, Ben,' he said.

'Nice to be here,' I said.

Mum, too, seemed even more cheerful than usual. It

might have had something do with discovering that, Mr Kemal, the man on the fresh fish counter at Sainsbury's, was Turkish. She'd got into the habit of popping in every day to brush up on her pronunciation. Dad and I were beginning to get sick of haddock and smoked mackerel.

On the other hand, it might have had something to do with the fact that Brad Piston had somehow survived his 300-metre death plunge with his teeth and suntan intact, and the fact that his mad brother had been locked up in a psychiatric prison.

Dad was happy. Mum was happy. I was happy. Mrs Breezeblock was threatening to come down on Barney, Jenks and me like a ton of bricks, but she didn't have a clue who we were.

Things were fab.

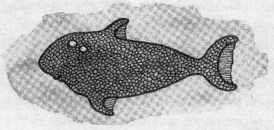

Anyway . . . after Breezeblock had finished lecturing us about throwing potatoes through car windows, the three of us trooped off to Mr Forsyth's room for another history lesson.

We had moved onto the Vikings now, and the Vikings were miles better than the Romans. They invaded every-one else's countries and built huge boats and burnt everything to the ground, rather than flouncing about making stupid aqueducts and wearing purple robes and having baths all the time.

'Staggering as it is,' said Mr Forsyth, as the lesson got going, 'the Vikings even managed to cross the Atlantic in their longships and reach America, which they named Vineland.'

'And Iceland, Sir,' I added, sticking my hand into the air and wagging it.

'Very good, Ben. Yes they did.' He seemed rather impressed.

'And they rowed all the way from Sweden and Norway down through the English Channel, to France and Spain,' I carried on, 'and they crossed Germany and rowed over Europe along the rivers and got as far as Constantinople which is in Turkey now and it's called Istanbul . . .'

It was all on account of the wall chart. Hanging above Presley's tank, I could see it when I was lying in bed. On the left-hand side, there was a picture of a Viking warrior wearing his horned helmet and fur cape, and a wooden hut and a longship in the background. On the right, there was this map of everywhere they went in their longships, from Constantinople to Iceland. And they didn't just go around burning everything to the ground. No. They used to trade in beer and salt and metal and wine, so they made loads and loads of money as well as burning everything to the ground, which sounded pretty cool to me.

Sometimes, dozing in bed at night, I used to imagine that I was in one of the longships, rowing through the thousand islands of the Skagerrak near Sweden. The seas would be rough, and the prow of the boat would be

cutting through the huge waves like a knife through butter. I'd be the Viking beating the big drum at the back of the boat, keeping everyone in time: thump, thump, thump; the salt spray in my hair, and my big beard flying in the wind.

Which is why I was able to impress Mr Forsyth so much. I don't think he had a Viking wall chart. I mean, he didn't know that it was the Vikings who supplied all the wax for the candles in the churches all across Europe, and so on.

So I shut up after a bit. I didn't want to make him look stupid. I didn't want to be out of his good books five minutes after I'd got into them again.

The other good news was that Fisty Morgan didn't seem to have twigged who had booby-trapped the toilets. Either he couldn't remember bumping into us minutes before it happened, or he didn't make the connection. He had laid into a couple of small boys from the year below one break time just to let off steam a bit, but that was nothing out of the ordinary. Agent Z's cover hadn't been blown.

Barney, Jenks and I had escaped certain death only on account of the smallness of Fisty Morgan's brain. We celebrated by turning the photocopied orang-utan picture into a dartboard, with a hundred point score for hitting him on the nose.

In short, with the exception of Presley, who was still refusing to touch his food, everything was brilliant.

# Armed with a Plastic Sheep

It was a couple of days later that things began to go seriously wrong.

We were standing in the school entrance hall, preparing for another Agent Z mission. The three mice Jenks had caught in his Dad's shed were safely tucked into his jacket pocket. Mr Lanchester knew nothing of the surprise that would be waiting for him when he got home that evening and opened his briefcase.

'O-way. A-kay,' said Barney. 'Atches-way ynchronise-say.'

'Oger-ray,' replied Jenks.

'Oger-ray,' I replied, rolling down my sleeve.

Which is when Jenks shouted, 'Look out!' and whipped into Barney's shadow.

'Ook-lay out-ay!' said Barney wearily. He seemed totally unruffled by Jenks' weird behaviour. 'Eak-spay in-ay ode-cay.'

'Stuff that!' Jenks wailed. 'Look!'

We looked in the direction of his shaking finger. Halfway down the main corridor, Fisty Morgan and his henchmen were making their way towards us. Jenks tried to sprint off towards the playground, but his jacket was held firmly in Barney's fist. He came to a sudden halt and was dragged backwards again.

'Relax,' hissed Barney. 'Why panic? We haven't done anything wrong, have we?'

'The fiver!' croaked Jenks. 'I owe him a fiver!'

'Oh . . .' replied Barney, realising too late.

By this time, Fisty was standing in front of us, his mates arranged in a semi-circle around him. He turned to Jenks.

'Ah, Jenkinson!' he said, just like Breezeblock says when she meets you in the corridor and you're in trouble for something or other. Except Fisty was more frightening than she was. She was only allowed to shout at you, or put you in detention. Fisty was allowed to do anything he liked.

'Yes?' quailed Jenks.

Barney and I stepped back, sensing danger.

'I seem to remember a little matter of that cash you owe me.'

'Really?' Jenks said, his voice warbling. 'Are you absolutely sure? Now let me see . . . When was this. . . ?' Jenks was playing for time. We were standing in the main entrance hall, after all. It could only be a matter of

72

seconds before a member of staff walked past. Then he would be safe. He would be able to make a break for it.

Fisty was playing for time, too. He liked it that way. Laying people out with one blow was a waste. He preferred to watch his victims squirm and sweat and plead. Then he'd lay them out with one blow.

No member of staff had appeared. With a twisted grin on his face, Fisty had begun nudging Jenks further and further back towards the wall. They were now almost hidden behind the Harvest Festival display that 3G had done to celebrate agriculture and farming and stuff.

I looked around the entrance hall. Fisty's lieutenants were moving into lookout positions near all the doors, watching out for oncoming staff. It looked like they'd trained for this sort of thing. It was not Jenks' lucky day.

'Maybe I should jog your memory a bit,' Fisty spat, moving his face so close to Jenks' that their noses were almost touching.

Barney and I watched helplessly as Fisty took his hands from his pockets, grabbed Jenks by the lapels and banged him hard against the wall.

'Remember now?' he grunted.

It was then that something extremely unfortunate happened.

Whilst grabbing Jenks' blazer, Fisty had put his hands on the secret Z badge pinned beneath the lapel. Pressing one hand against Jenks' chest to hold him in the corner, he slowly tore it off and turned it over in his hands.

'Z?' he said to himself.

We could almost hear the cogs in his simple but violent brain ticking over towards the inevitable, horrible conclusion.

'Agent Z . . .,' he said, the light beginning to dawn. 'Where have I heard that before. . . ? The toilet. . . !'

The awful truth suddenly clicked, and Fisty went berserk. 'You piece of filth!' he screamed at Jenks, spittle bubbling at the corners of his mouth.

Seething with anger, he turned round to grab anything he could use to clobber Jenks with. The only thing within reach was the Harvest Festival display. Luckily this consisted mostly of carrots and broccoli, a plastic sheep, a vase of flowers and a bale of hay. Unluckily, it also contained a full-sized garden spade and fork thrust into a bucket of earth.

Purple with rage, Fisty leant backwards, grabbed the fork, pushed Jenks back against the wall and shoved the prongs up against his neck. It seemed quite likely that Jenks was going to be murdered.

It all happened in a nanosecond. Barney looked at me. I looked at Barney. It was suicide, but we had no choice.

Barney said, 'Go for it!' and we went for it. Together, we ran at Fisty. Barney grabbed the garden spade and swung it high into the air like a pick-axe. I grabbed hold of the plastic sheep and lunged it at the back of Fisty's head.

Which is exactly the position that Mr Forsyth found us in.

'Stop that!' he roared.

We froze as we were. He walked round the Harvest Festival display and stood looking at us. Jenks was lying slumped against the wall with the garden fork shoved under his chin. Fisty was lying semi-conscious on top of Jenks with the garden fork in his hands. I was crouching over Fisty holding a broken plastic sheep. And Barney was standing, like a knight crusader on a medieval battlefield, the spade held above his head like a broadsword.

The three mice, who had had enough of this, slipped out of Jenks' pocket, and hot footed it towards the hay bale in the Harvest festival display.

We were in hot water, make no mistake. The water was especially hot on account of the fact that things looked a bit ambiguous from where Mr Forsyth was standing. From his point of view, it might well have seemed as if Barney and I had simply decided to knock Fisty Morgan's brains out, or that all three of us had decided to murder Jenks.

The problem was that Mr Forsyth had been in the school for only two terms. Any other teacher would have known instantly what had happened. Any other teacher would have known that no pupils in their right minds would attack Fisty. Any other teacher would have known that if Fisty was involved in any trouble whatsoever, he must have started it.

But Mr Forsyth was the sort of teacher who made a point of 'not being prejudiced'. We were all under suspicion. 'Into my room,' he barked. 'Now!'

Come to think of it, Mr Forsyth shouldn't have been a teacher at all. He should have been in the army. He was the spitting image of those British officers you see in First

World War films. On the surface, they're perfectly polite and gentlemanly. They have tea with the vicar's daughter and read poetry in bed at night. But underneath, they're stark-staring bonkers. They just can't wait to run through a hail of gunfire shouting *God Save the Queen.*

This wasn't a bad thing really. If there is one thing close to the hearts of stark-staring mad British army officers it is 'fair play'. Other teachers might not have bothered wasting energy finding out who did what to whom and why, and simply bunged us all in detention. This, however, would not have been 'fair play'. So Mr Forsyth listened carefully to each of our stories in turn. And it was during Jenks' version that things started to hot up a bit.

'Anyway,' said Jenks, 'a couple of weeks ago, Morgan said he'd kick my head in if I didn't give him five quid . . .'

As he said these words, something flipped inside Mr Forsyth's head. Beating up smaller boys to make them give you their pocket money was certainly not 'fair play' by any stretch of the imagination. It was despicable. It was cowardly. It was mean. It certainly wasn't something a self-respecting British Army officer would allow to happen – no way.

Mr Forsyth's eyes became narrow and started to glaze over. He got up from his desk and circled Fisty Morgan several times before asking, 'Is this true?'

Fisty kept his mouth shut and his eyes pointing straight ahead of him. After all, he was the boy who had been suspended for punching Mr Lanchester. He wasn't going to be intimidated *that* easily.

'I'm going to ask you one more time,' repeated Mr Forsyth in a voice so calm it was eerie. 'Is this true? Did you tell Jenkinson to give you a fiver or you would kick his head in?'

Fisty neither moved nor spoke.

Barney, Jenks and I hotched nervously from one foot to the other. Slowly, Mr Forsyth circled Fisty a few more times like a leopard circling a rump steak. Finally he came to a halt standing behind Fisty's back.

What we could see, and what Fisty couldn't see, was Mr Forsyth reaching silently over to his desk and picking up his long, metal, metre ruler. He stretched his arm in front of him to loosen up his muscles, then flexed the ruler between his hands to make sure it was good and springy.

The ruler trick was coming right up.

Fisty was miles away, staring out of the window and across the playing fields. We were bracing ourselves for the explosion that was about to come, and Mr Forsyth was lifting the metal ruler high above his head.

He took a step backwards, lifted one foot off the ground, and wound his arm backwards like Xiao-Xiao Ptoing setting the Chinese all-comers record for the javelin. Then he let rip, bringing the ruler down at something near the speed of light.

It passed within an inch of Fisty's ear and struck the edge of the desk with such force that it split the top into two pieces. The noise was so loud, I saw a little cluster of stars swimming in front of my eyes for at least a minute afterwards.

Fisty screamed. He actually screamed. It was wonderful and terrifying and hilarious at the same time.

'I asked you a question, Morgan,' said Mr Forsyth, in the same terrifyingly calm voice, 'and I think it would be a good idea if you answered me. Is this true?'

I noticed, to my surprise, that Fisty was still shaking. 'It was only five quid, Sir,' he gabbled suddenly.

'You . . . are . . . pathetic,' sighed Mr Forsyth wearily.

Silence fell on the room. Forsyth lowered his head and walked to his desk and back, rubbing his chin and thinking hard. Having returned to Fisty he snapped to attention and barked 'Right. . . !'

Fisty jumped a mile. He must have thought Forsyth was going to knock his teeth out. He stumbled backwards, tripped on a broken piece of desk and somersaulted over a stray chair.

Then Forsyth said, 'The Head's office. Now.' Fisty stood and shambled into the corridor like a beaten dog. 'You lot,' added Forsyth, pausing at the door, 'stay here.'

When we heard the two of them turn the corner at the end of the corridor, Barney threw his head back and let out a wild coyote-yelp of joy. 'Yeeeee-haaaa!'

'Magic, magic, magic, magic . . .' Jenks chanted.

We'd never seen anything like it. For as long as we could remember, Fisty had been a law unto himself. The teachers were as scared of him as most of the kids were. He had never done any work he didn't want to do. He had never answered a question he didn't want to answer. He skipped half his lessons and he had certainly never turned up for detention.

And now he had been reduced to a shivering wreck and was being herded along the corridor towards Breeze-block's office. It was like Christmas times ten.

We were still laughing with relief when Mr Forsyth came back into the room. Only then did it occur to us that we might be in for similar treatment. We fell instantly silent and stood to attention as if we were on his personal parade ground.

'I'll deal with you lot myself,' he said briskly, sitting down at his desk and scribbling something on a piece of paper. When the note was finished, he handed it to Barney, and said, 'That's my address. I want you in my garden, eight-thirty, Saturday morning.'

'What?' said Jenks, stupidly. 'Uh?'

'Shut up!' I hissed under my breath.

Mr Forsyth walked to the window, stared out into the distance and put his hands together behind his back. After a few minutes, he explained, 'No point in getting you suspended. That'll only put you behind with your work. And detention seems to have no effect on you whatsoever. On the other hand, a few hours' hard labour might just knock some sense into your thick heads. I shall write to your parents informing them of this.'

We looked at one another in confusion.

'Now, if you don't mind,' he said, ending the conversation, 'I have some work to be getting on with.'

I was livid. We hadn't done anything wrong. In fact, when Forsyth found us, we were risking our lives to save a friend from certain death. It seemed a bit rich to punish us by making us dig his garden. What we deserved were medals.

Mum was sympathetic. She said Forsyth sounded like a rough old stick. But Dad totally failed to see my point.

'Sounds alright to me,' he said. 'I just don't understand what the problem is.'

'The problem . . .' I spluttered. 'The problem . . .'

'The problem what?' he replied.

'The problem is . . . he can't make us do his garden for him, can he?' I continued, 'and at the weekend, too?'

'It seems like he can,' countered Dad. 'And why not? I'd just count yourself lucky that you didn't get thrashed.'

'They can't cane people anymore, Dad,' I explained.

'Honestly,' he grunted, 'you lot have it easy these days.'

'Dad!' I said, beginning to get seriously irritated.

We didn't get the chance to have a full-blown argument. At precisely that moment, Mum swept into the lounge, put down her indoor watering can, took her liqueur chocolates from the cupboard, poured a glass of sherry, settled herself onto the sofa, excavated the remote control from under the cushions and announced, 'Silence!' It was *Love Hotel* time.

'Not that garbage?' I whined.

'Ben . . .' she explained carefully. 'Compared to listening to you two bickering at each other, *Love Hotel* is high art. Now, shoosh.'

'Dad?' I whispered.

'What, Ben?' he whispered wearily back.

'Will you take Presley to the vet for me?'

'Sure thing, partner,' agreed Dad, giving me the O.K. sign.

'Oi, you two!' shouted Mum. 'Shut up or clear out!'

We cleared out.

# Slave Labour

The legion of Killer Crabs were only ten miles from the outskirts of London now. They had clicked and snapped and munched their way across two hundred miles of countryside, turning people and pets and trees and cattle into crunchy crab-snacks, and leaving a trail of bones in their wake.

High up on Marlow Hill, Agent Z parted the long grass and pressed the binoculars to his eyes. Below him, the army of hard, red shells was trooping remorselessly up the valley. Light was beginning to fade. Evening was finally coming on. It was now or never. Agent Z took his walkie-talkie from his combat jacket and ordered the screens to be moved into position.

The three hundred men from the Queen's Royal

Hussars took up the strain on the ropes and began winching. The vast poles started to lift skyward, the monstrous canvases stretching tight between them. Through his binoculars, Agent Z was able to see similar canvases being erected on the far side of the valley.

He glanced back down towards the Killer Crabs. They had looked up briefly at the bizarre objects taking shape on the hills around them, then simply looked away. Perhaps they were short-sighted. Perhaps they had plans of their own. Perhaps they arrogantly thought that nothing whatsoever could stop them. Maybe they were right. It was a possibility Agent Z did not want to consider.

Lifting the walkie-talkie again, he ordered the military commanders to start the generators and connect the amplifiers.

A wall of solid, grey cloud slid suddenly across the sun, darkening the entire landscape. The crabs' luck was running out at last. Agent Z crossed his fingers and began the countdown. 'Ten . . . Nine . . . Eight . . .' He looked behind him and saw a heavily armoured Land-Rover pull up. 'Seven . . . Six . . .' A door opened and the Prime Minister stepped out onto the wet grass, dressed in a bullet-proof windcheater. 'Five . . . Four . . .'

He saw the Prime Minister give him a thumbs-up sign and mouth the words, 'We're counting on you.'

Agent Z gritted his teeth. This was their only chance. This was their last chance. 'Three . . . Two . . . Head-phones on . . . One . . . Ignition!'

There was a huge crackle as a million watts of electricity surged into the heavy-duty equipment; then an ear-splitting 'Whump!' as the theme music began. High above their heads, the screens lit up and the credits began to roll.

Down in the valley, the Killer Crabs at last began to take notice. Their antennae frenetically swept the horizon, desperately trying to work out the reason for the vile din which was buffeting their crab-ears from all directions.

They stopped in their tracks. They knew something was wrong. They knew something was very, very wrong. Whether they could read the words 'Love Hotel' projected in day-glo pink on the screens all around them, it was impossible to say. But there was no denying their screams of horror as this week's espisode began and they were treated to vast, multi-vision shots of Brad Piston and Lucinda Diamond snogging in his hospital bed. 'Marry me, Lucinda. Marry me and half the Love Hotel will be yours forever. Yes, forever.'

The screens showed a horrifying close-up of Brad Piston's suntanned, grinning face. Agent Z and the men from the Queen's Royal Hussars shielded their eyes. For a few seconds, the crabs were confused, not knowing which way to turn. Then, as one, still screaming with horror, the vast crustacean crowd turned on their shelly heels in the falling light, and began crawling as fast as their claws would carry them, away from the valley, away from *Love Hotel*, away from London, and back towards the sea. Within six hours the Killer Crabs had disappeared beneath the surf never to show their claws again.

'The people of this country,' said the Prime Minister, gripping Agent Z's cool, steady hand, 'will never be able to repay you for what you've done today.'

I was daydreaming again. Life was scummy. Daydreams were all that Agent Z was fit for any longer.

Fisty Morgan had been suspended, true, but only for three weeks. In no time at all, he was going to be back at school. Worse, he now knew for certain who had sabotaged the toilets. Barney, Jenks and I were going to be numbers one, two and three on his hit list. And, to add insult to injury, the three of us were going to be used as slave-labour by Mr Forsyth.

We'd somehow lost the taste for undercover operations.

'Stop whinging,' said Dad, shooing me off from the door at the crack of dawn on Saturday morning. 'It'll only take a few hours. Just remember, your Mr Forsyth could have called in the police and had you done for G.B.H.'

'Yes, Dad,' I groaned and dragged myself down the path.

The thing was, Dad didn't know Mr Forsyth, whereas we did. Mind you, we didn't know anything about his garden. We were in for a bit of a shock.

The Crew met up at the Command Centre and hurled a few darts into Fisty's face to cheer ourselves up. We then reluctantly made our way to Mr Forsyth's house. By chance, it turned out to be one of the newly built ones on the Crane Grove Estate, next to the park.

We had no idea what we were letting ourselves in for. In our minds, we had pictured a garden rather like Mr

Forsyth himself: lots of neat, straight lines; a square flowerbed or two; a strip of lawn; some tough shrubs; a solid, manly sort of garden. So, we were more than a little surprised when he led us through his kitchen and out onto a strip of land which looked, more than anything, like a World War Two bomb site.

'I've just moved in, you see,' he explained, handing out spades and gloves. 'So I haven't really had a chance to clear the place, what with coaching the athletics team and marking your homework . . .'

There were piles of bricks. There was a rusty, steel fence dividing the area in two. There were the remains of a rotted garden shed and a wrought-iron bench. On top of this, it looked as if the previous owners had got rid of all their household garbage by simply hurling it out of the back door. There was not a blade of grass in sight; nor a clump of earth for that matter; just trash, knee-deep trash.

'O.K. Here's what I want you to do,' he ordered. 'You see that skip in the alley behind the wall? I want everything dumped in there. Everything. By the end of the afternoon, I want to be able to look out of the window and see a nice, flat rectangle of earth.' He checked his watch. 'The first shift will last till ten o'clock. Then we break for tea.'

It was an hour later that we unearthed the escape pod. We had shifted a pile of bricks and were levelling the ground underneath. Suddenly, Barney thrust his blade more deeply than usual and struck a solid, metal object. He called us over and we began removing the earth from around it with our bare hands.

It was the shape of an egg, but much larger, a metre or so from end to end. Although it must have been buried for many years, the surface was still smooth and polished – a glassy, smoke-grey metal.

When we had dug a pit around the object, we were able to roll it over. On its reverse was a small panel of lights and buttons set into a transparent screen. As we were turning it, one of the small lights had begun to flash.

Jenks reached forward and laid a finger on one of the buttons. There was a soft, whirring noise and a hatch in the front of the pod began to swing slowly open, like the door of a very expensive car. We stood back, terrified.

The hatch came to a halt and, inside, we were able to see a creature strapped to a soft, rubber seat surrounded by dials and switches and computer screens. The creature had long, knobbled limbs, the colour and texture of walnuts. On either side of its long, fanged snout, were two

bubble-eyes, closed under leathery lids. We held our breath as the eyes levered themselves open.

'Greetings,' announced the creature in a harsh, gargling voice. 'You are the Finders. I have waited many long and tedious years for your arrival . . .'

O.K., so there wasn't an escape pod. Which was a pity, really. If we *had* found an alien escape pod, it would have been the only interesting thing which happened all day.

By ten o'clock, we could barely move. Our arms and legs were aching and we were out of breath. Working alongside us, Mr Forsyth had had no such problems. He whistled and chatted constantly, as if he was enjoying every moment of the back-breaking task. He must have been mad.

'I must say, you boys are doing the most magnificent job!' declared Mrs Forsyth when she came out of the house at ten o'clock, balancing a tray of tea and biscuits. 'I am *most* impressed.'

She ought to have been impressed. It would have cost Mr Forsyth hundreds of pounds to get workmen in to do what we were doing for free. I wondered whether she was going to be so impressed when the first one of us died during the afternoon of a heart attack brought on by overwork.

Apparently, the biscuits were extremely good – home-made brandy snaps and shortbread. Barney told me so. I'd have liked to judge for myself, but he got to the tray first.

'Well, I hope that teaches you a lesson,' said Mr Forsyth as we handed over the spades and gloves and prepared to leave at the end of the afternoon.

'Yes, sir,' we droned in bored, exhausted voices.

'And of course,' he smiled, 'thank you very much for all your hard work.'

It seemed a bit rich, thanking us for something he'd forced us to do. Not that we were going to mention this. But, yes, it had taught us a lesson. The lesson was that if Fisty Morgan tried to murder one of us again, we should let him carry on and do it. Otherwise, Mr Forsyth would do his best to murder us instead, by other means.

Jenks had cricked his back. Barney had got himself a long gash on the palm of his hand, and I had a constant, dull pain throbbing in every muscle.

'See you in history on Monday, chaps!' Mr Forsyth beamed cheerfully as we left through the front door.

We dragged our weary feet down the road, waited till he had returned indoors, then found the nearest gap in the fence. We squeezed through and headed onto the wasteground towards the Command Centre to recover.

'I am shattered!' I moaned.

'Snap,' said Barney.

'We ought to tell the headmistress, you know,' Jenks suggested.

'Tell her what?' I asked.

'Tell her that one of her teachers tortures kids,' explained Jenks. 'That he makes them do his dirty work for him.'

'Give over, Jenks,' I groaned. I was too tired to argue. 'One: Breezeblock will probably think it's a brilliant idea. Two: I couldn't care less. Just leave it, O.K.?'

'But . . .' Jenks wouldn't leave it.

'Barney?' I turned towards the window to get Barney's support. 'Tell Jenks, will you?'

But Barney didn't answer. The binoculars were pressed to his eyes and he was deep in concentration. 'Come over here,' he beckoned us. 'You might like to take a look at this.'

We got up and walked over, our ravaged muscles making us plod like old men. Barney handed me the binoculars.

'Just to the left of that oak tree,' he said, putting his hands on the binoculars and manoeuvring them for me. 'See that chink of street light? Through there.'

I gazed into the chink of light. We could see the back of Mr Forsyth's Vauxhall Chevette, parked outside his garage. 'So? What about it?'

Barney walked over to the fridge and cracked open a can of coke. 'One last operation,' he nodded seriously, swigging from the can. 'Then we liquidate Agent Z.'

Back at home, Dad was watching the *Jailhouse Rock* video. Mum was putting horrible, pink buttons on the horrible pink cardigan for Mad Aunt Gwen's daughter, and doing lesson number 72.

'Ormanlarimizi keçilere yediriyoruz . . .' she was saying as I came in. 'Ben, petal, you *do* look a state!'

I did, too. There was mud on my face. I had torn the sleeve of my shirt and the blisters were starting to come up on my fingers. I was owed a lot of sympathy.

'Run yourself a bath and I'll do you a hot drink, alright?'

In the end, then, it wasn't so bad after all. I got supper in bed and a large mug of hot chocolate. Added to which, Mum also put her black-and-white bedside television on my chest of drawers for the evening.

'And I've booked Presley in for a check up with the vet on Wednesday,' Dad added, 'if he doesn't mind waiting till then.'

'That'll be fine,' I replied. 'Presley's good at waiting.'

So, with a weight off my mind, I watched *The Guns of Navarone* then fell into a deep sleep, dreaming of the Ultimate Operation.

# The Kipper Job

I found the kippers buried deep in the chest freezer at the back of the garage. They came in blocks of ten, which was more than enough. I wrapped one block in a Sainsbury's bag and shoved them underneath the dustbin so I could pick them up on the way to the Command Centre later in the day.

They wouldn't be missed. Since Mum had got matey with Mr Kemal, she had filled the freezer with enough fish to last the three of us through a nuclear war.

And if they *were* missed? No matter. I'd face the music when the time came. The mission was too important to let personal worries get in the way. It was a matter of honour. And revenge. And the worst smell we could get our hands on.

'Okey-dokey!' announced Barney, pulling a large book from inside his jacket and laying it on the table next to the Beverley Sisters' mints. 'The *Hayes Manual* for the Chevette.'

'Where did you get that?' asked Jenks.

'My Uncle Bernie's got a Chevette, too. I borrowed it for the day.' He flicked through the manual until he found a cut-away diagram of the engine compartment. 'Now, this is the exhaust manifold,' he explained, jabbing his fat forefinger at the centre of the picture. 'It gets good and hot and, what's more, it's not too big. We should be able to get wire round it fairly easily. Jenks, you got the wire O.K.?'

'Sure,' confirmed Jenks, pulling from the pocket of his jeans a cat's cradle of fuse wires of assorted lengths and thicknesses.

'This is where it's going to go.' Barney biroed a circle round the picture of the manifold. 'Remember that, and take a good look at the diagram, Ben. It's going to be dark, you're going to be lying on your back and we're going to have to be quick. We have to know what we're doing. Precisely.'

'Me?' I said. 'Now, just hang on a minute . . .'

Barney shrugged his shoulders. 'I'm too fat, and he's too stupid. Ben . . . you're our man.'

We moved out just after dusk. We crept silently to the wire fence at the edge of the waste ground and gazed into the gloom. The Chevette was still parked on the drive and the Forsyths' house lights were on. Perfect.

We slipped through the tear in the metal netting and walked round the back of the estate till we reached the alleyway that ran behind the gardens. As soon as we were off the road, Jenks moved into a crouching position and hid himself in the shadow of the wall.

'What on earth are you doing?' hissed Barney.

'Hiding,' Jenks replied.

'Get up, you dork!' Barney grabbed his shoulder and hoisted him back to his feet. 'Don't go making yourself look suspicious. Get casual!'

Thirty metres down the alley, we found the skip we had filled the previous day. As planned, we gave Jenks a foot-up onto it then sauntered casually round the estate while he did the surveillance. On our return, he was waiting under the eves of a nearby shed. The three of us walked silently to the road again before talking.

'O.K.' said Jenks. 'There was only a crack in the curtain, but they're both in there. I'm certain.'

'You were right, Ben,' smiled Barney.

'Yeh,' I said. 'International athletics. England V. Italy. Eight-thirty. I knew he wouldn't miss it.'

'Right then . . .' grinned Jenks eagerly.

'Action stations,' said Barney.

'Actions-way ations-stay!' whispered Jenks.

'Very good,' said Barney, patting him on the head like a well-behaved dog. 'Very good.'

We split up.

I checked the kippers and the wire and crept round to the front of the house. I waited by the garden wall till the coast was clear, then rolled backwards onto the flower-bed, under the hedge and across to the car.

The other two were going to remain on look out — Jenks at the back and Barney out the front across the road. How they might be able to help if things went wrong, I didn't know, but it seemed like the professional thing to do.

It was a lot harder than I thought it was going to be. In the *Hayes Manual*, the diagram of the Chevette engine looked straightforward. But it was now pitch dark under the chassis. I was lying on my back and every piece of metal over my head was covered in oil and dirt and rust.

It reminded me of the time we'd discussed frogs in Biology. We'd looked at the diagrams of the frog's insides the week before so that we'd know the names of all the bits and what they did; but when we sliced open the fat, green belly there was just blood and gunge and bony bits and tubey bits. You couldn't tell the liver from the colon, or the kidney from the stomach.

Fumbling in the dark, I found the oil sump on the bottom of the main engine block and, as my eyes became accustomed to the dark, I was able to make out the branching outline of the manifold.

I extracted the Sainsbury's bag from my jacket, took out five of the kippers and wedged them between two of the

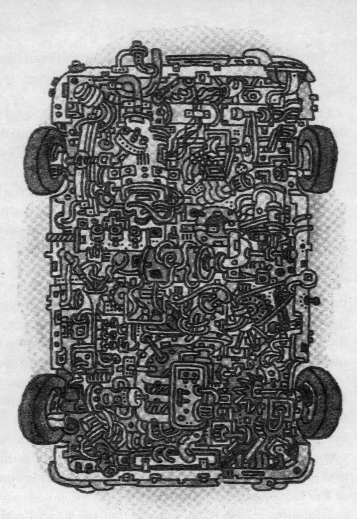

tubes. Holding them with one hand, I unravelled a length of fuse wire and threaded it round the manifold, pulling the fish tight against the metal and twisting the ends together to fasten it.

The first wire was too thin. It sliced into the fish and it

sliced into my thumb. The greasy fish oil got into the cut and hurt like crazy. I bit my tongue and finished the job with the rest of the thicker wire.

When I'd finished, I picked the broken bits of fish from my face and off the concrete, put them into the bag with the remaining kippers and slid it back into my jacket. It had worked like a dream. Now it was time to vanish. I began wriggling towards the side of the car.

Which is when the car alarm went off.

I had caught the zip of my jacket on a protruding bolt and, as I tugged to get it free, I had rocked the car slightly from side to side. Without any warning, a piercing siren began screaming centimetres away from my face.

I jumped in fright, banged my head on the underside of the car, doubled up on account of the pain and whacked my knees on something hard and pointy. Only when I slumped back onto the tarmac did I notice the sweat of fear beginning to trickle down my face. I had begun to shake. Somewhere behind my head, I heard the click of a front door opening.

I was trapped.

Mr Forsyth's footsteps rang out on the drive as he walked to the passenger door of the car. I pulled my feet up and pressed my arms against my sides, willing myself to be invisible. The car door opened, he leant in, flicked a switch and the alarm shut off as he closed the door. I waited for him to turn and head back to the house, but he didn't. He just stood there, waiting, listening, looking.

I turned my head a fraction towards where he was standing. I had never taken much notice of Mr Forsyth's shoes before. But I was taking a lot of notice of them now – in glorious, microscopic close-up: big, brown, lace-up brogues with steel heel-tabs which gave off tiny sparks in the darkness as he shifted his feet. He was wearing green corduroy trousers and checkered socks.

Sweat was running into my eyes. My knees and forehead were still zinging with pain. Where was Barney? Where was Jenks? They must have heard the alarm go off. They must have seen Mr Forsyth come out of the house.

I tried to remember the Agent Z Emergency Escape Plan for The Ultimate Operation and realised, to my distress, that there wasn't one. I breathed as quietly and as little as possible. Seconds began to seem like fortnights. I was beginning to feel dizzy. Suddenly, a voice shot out of the darkness. 'Hey you!'

It was coming from somewhere down the street – a menacing, threatening, drunken voice. Forsyth's feet turned towards the direction of the noise.

'Yes, that's right, you,' the voice insisted. 'You with the snotty jacket and the corduroys, pal!'

'Who is that?' barked Mr Forsyth.

'Never you mind,' answered the voice, 'you toffee-nosed git!'

'Come here and say that, you cheeky oik!' challenged Mr Forsyth, walking to the end of the drive.

'No. You come here and I'll say it your face, you yellow-bellied little toe-rag!'

Unable to take the insults any longer, Mr Forsyth had started marching down the street towards the cheeky oik, rolling up his sleeves and preparing to administer a bit of rough justice. Whoever was shouting at him would probably be laying turf in his garden the following weekend.

I had been saved by the mysterious stranger.

I slipped out from under the car, ducked beneath the hedge, jumped back onto the pavement and scooted away in the other direction.

'That was close,' I gasped, collapsing on the sofa in the Command Centre. 'That was *really* close.'

'Brilliant work,' said Jenks, shaking my hand.

'Did you hear that bloke,' I continued, 'slagging off Forsyth in the middle of the street? It was only because of him that I managed to get away.'

'No,' confessed Jenks. 'I was round the back all the time.'

'It was amazing,' I explained. 'I mean, I was lying there under the car with him standing right next to me and then this guy starts shouting . . .'

Barney walked over, leaned close to my face, jabbed his finger against the end of my nose and said, in a surprisingly deep and menacing voice, 'Hey! You with the snotty jacket and the corduroys, pal! Yes, you, you toffee-nosed git. . . !'

'Barney!' I said, staggered. 'It was *you*!'

Smiling, he buffed his nails on his jacket and blew on them. 'Yep . . . Agent Z Spur-Of-The-Moment Emergency Escape Plan No. 436 . . . Never fails.'

# Stinky

It was brilliant. Forsyth stank to high heaven.

Barney, Jenks and I were standing at the corner of the playground waiting for the beginning of assembly. Thankfully, we weren't talking about the Ultimate Operation at the time. We were feeling a bit superstitious, and it seemed to be tempting fate to congratulate ourselves before we'd been able to assess the full effects.

Instead, Jenks was showing us the Swiss army penknife he'd bought on Saturday with the money from his paper round. It was the business: two straight blades, a saw, scissors, wire-stripper, cork-screw, can-opener, the tweezers, the getting-stones-out-from-horses-hooves-thing. I made a mental note to put one on my Christmas present list. He was just demonstrating the toothpick when Mr Forsyth walked up behind us.

'So, you survived your spot of gardening, then?' he said, turning to Barney. 'How's the hand, by the way?'

Barney showed him his palm, a blood-stained elastoplast wrapped around it.

'You'll live,' smiled Mr Forsyth. 'It doesn't look as if gangrene has set in.'

The reek of kippers billowed off Forsyth's clothes. Either the fish had warmed up so slowly on the manifold that he hadn't noticed the stench mounting inside the car, or he had noticed and was trying to play it as cool as possible.

'Sir?' said Barney.

'Go on . . .' replied Mr Forsyth.

'I'm not being rude, Sir, but . . .' Barney looked strangely nervous. It wasn't like him at all.

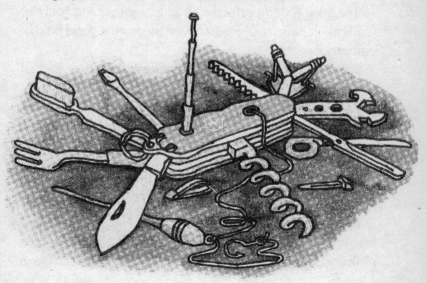

'But what?' said Mr Forsyth, genuinely curious.

I started to worry. Barney was going to mention the smell. I wanted to stop him, but I couldn't say anything without blowing the gaffe.

And then it clicked. I should have trusted him. Forsyth stank of fish. You couldn't help noticing it. The suspicious thing would have been *not* to mention it.

'Well, Sir,' continued Barney, 'if you don't mind me saying so, you smell of seaweed, or prawns or something.'

Seaweed or prawns. That was a nice touch.

Mr Forsyth raised his nose in the air, widened his nostrils and sniffed like a bloodhound. He then lifted the end of his tie and smelled it microscopically.

'You're right.' He agreed, knotting his eyebrows and shaking his head. 'How extraordinary!'

'Sorry, Sir,' apologised Barney, 'I didn't mean to . . .'

'No, no, that's perfectly alright,' replied Mr Forsyth, 'and thank you. You've just saved me from a good deal of embarrassment.'

So, he hadn't noticed after all. Either that or he had an Olympic gold metal in playing it cool.

As he walked away, the pressure of suppressed giggles in our lungs increased till we thought our heads would explode. Only when we saw his stiff-backed silhouette disappearing through the staff room door, did we bolt round the corner and let out great burping snorts of laughter.

Before assembly began, Mr Forsyth had changed into his athletics tracksuit. Up on the stage, the fluorescent pink and green of his flashy waterproofing stood out like a sore thumb amongst the gravy-brown cardigans and battle-grey skirts.

Moreover, when Breezeblock gave us all a short lecture about wearing the proper school uniform, and not putting coloured socks on under our black trousers and so forth, a low, cheeky whistle went round the entire hall. I think I saw Mr Forsyth's ears go red, but he was a long way off, so I couldn't be sure.

I was on top of the world. Agent Z had successfully carried out his last and most glorious mission. We were the champions, make no mistake. Later that day, there would be a new addition to the Command Centre notice board, reading:

<u>The Kipper Job</u>
Daring – 10/10
Success – 10/10
Laugh Value – 10/10

Life was wonderful. Everything seemed to have a rosy glow around it for the rest of the school day. Even science was fun.

'And water is made up of oxygen and hydrogen,' I answered. 'Its formula is $H_2O$.'

'Is copper an element?' I asked. 'And iron?'

'Coal is made of carbon,' I offered.

'When things burn they join up with the atoms of oxygen,' I explained. 'Neon is a gas and you get it inside striplights . . . Salt is made of chlorine and sodium . . .'

On and on I went. There was no stopping me. I was a

star. If I could carry out sophisticated undercover operations for Agent Z, then I could do atoms and elements standing on my head wearing a blindfold.

The three of us were still buzzing when we ran onto the football field for a friendly against St Benedict's. Needless to say, we made mincemeat of them. Barney stayed on the pitch for the entire game, mowing his way through the opposing team like a Sherman tank, and Jenks weaved in and out of their defenders like a mad ferret, tackling one of them with such ferocity that he had to be carried off on a stretcher.

And me? It was as if we'd built a brick wall across the mouth of the goal. Nothing got past me, however high, however fast, however swerving. As soon as the ball left the boot of a St Benedict's player, I sprang into the air and flew like a bird, my infallible hands snatching it in mid-air or punching it clear over the bar.

We trounced them fourteen-nil.

'What got into you three, then?' asked Mr Lanchester, after the game, trying not to look impressed.

'We were just biding our time,' said Barney, 'waiting for the right moment to demonstrate our true skill.'

Mr Forsyth clearly hadn't twigged the source of the fish smell.

That afternoon he had got back into the kippered car and driven five boys over to the sports complex at Greenbridge for a county athletics trial. The kipper pong had obviously got into his tracksuit, because, at about four o'clock, we caught sight of him walking along the corridor to the school library wearing one of the 1920s' suits left over from the Drama Soc's Christmas production of *The Great Gatsby*. He must have borrowed it, having nothing else to wear that did not reek of fish.

Even the imminent return of Fisty Morgan didn't worry us any more. After all, it was Agent Z who had sabotaged the car of the man who had reduced Fisty to a quivering wreck. We were invincible.

Or so we thought.

Later on in the day, something rather peculiar happened.

I had just got in from school. I was taking a couple of digestives from the biscuit tin in the kitchen and removing my tie when Mum came into the room.

'This is for you, apparently,' she announced, handing me a small, white envelope.

'Oh,' I said. 'Thanks.'

I turned it over in my hands. On the front of the unstamped envelope were written the words: 'For the attention of Agent Z', in letters carefully cut from a newspaper. Whilst Mum busied herself at the sink, I opened it and unfolded the enclosed letter. This, too, was written in the same newspaper lettering. It said:

'Dear Agent Z,

Be at the Command Centre at
seven o'clock sharp tonight.
Ignore this invitation at your
peril. You have been warned.

The Masked Crusader.'

My first thought was that this was another of Barney's schemes. Perhaps, now that Agent Z was going to be liquidated, he had decided that the Masked Crusader should take his place. And why not? It would be a pity to play no more practical jokes, after all. Perhaps, on the other hand, Barney just enjoyed cutting up newspapers and sending mysterious messages.

Which was when a slightly disturbing thought struck me. 'Mum?' I asked.

'What, love?' she said.

'When did this arrive?'

'Now let me think,' she mused, chiselling the remains of the Yorkshire pudding off a baking tray. 'Yes. I was repotting the geraniums and there was this fascinating Open University programme on the TV about crocodiles which, apparently, are the nearest living relatives to the brontosaurus. So . . . ooh . . . about three o'clock-ish.'

'Did you see who delivered it?' I quizzed her.

'No.'

'Didn't you go outside and see who it was?'

'Of course, Ben,' she replied, giving me a funny look. 'I always run out into the street when something comes through the letterbox.'

'Yeh. Sorry,' I said.

I did some hard thinking. Barney, Jenks and I had played football from half-past two till half-past three. Then we'd been together in the changing rooms for the next half-hour or so. It was over a mile from school to our house. Even if you ran, it would have taken you ten minutes.

Either Mum's memory was going to pieces or there was something seriously wrong.

# Introducing . . . The Masked Crusader

I rang Barney and Jenks. They'd both got home to find similar notes waiting for them. Or so they said.

I whinged at Mum until she let me take Badger out for a late walk. As agreed, we then met up at the roundabout in the park just before seven. I let Badger loose and shooed away a couple of small kids so that we could have a serious discussion in private. I made Barney and Jenks swear on their Z badges, then asked them, on their word of honour, whether either of them had sent the notes.

'Not me,' said Barney.

'Scout's honour,' agreed Jenks.

So, Mum's memory had been fine. Something was seriously wrong.

'Look,' I said, bringing up the possibility that had been

worrying me for the last three hours, 'could it be Fisty? I mean, is it just possible. . . ?'

'Fisty . . . I'd never thought . . . Oh my God!' said Jenks, chewing his fingers, getting up off the roundabout and pacing in small circles. 'We're in big trouble, ultra-mega-big trouble.'

Barney shook his head slowly. 'Chill out,' he said to Jenks, forcing him to sit down again. 'How would he know about the Command Centre?'

'But what if . . . I mean . . . couldn't he. . . ?' Jenks flapped.

'Think about it,' said Barney.

But Jenks was not in a thinking sort of mood. 'Brenda knows about it,' he said.

Barney roared with laughter.

'Come off it,' I groaned. 'Your little sister couldn't even spell "The Masked Crusader". Besides, I thought she was terrified of the Beverley Sisters . . .'

Jenks sat shaking his head idiotically, and we fell into a deep silence. Finally, Barney began nodding seriously, and said, in a dark voice, 'There's no other alternative, then.'

'What?' snapped Jenks, nervously.

'We . . .' said Barney, winking secretly at me and smiling, 'are entering the realm of . . . the supernatural.'

'Shut up,' I said quietly.

It was hard seeing anything funny about the situation; and, to make matters worse, the light was fading.

All too soon, seven o'clock arrived. Our three watches agreed, so there was no disputing the fact.

If Barney was scared, he wasn't showing it. On the contrary, he seemed to be enjoying our discomfort. 'Zero hour,' he said. 'Let's get this over and done with.'

Reluctantly, we stood and followed him to the wasteground.

Five minutes later, we were standing by the covered cellar window at the back of the Command Centre. We had peered through every crack in the boarded-up windows, but could see nothing. It looked just as it had always done. There were no clues as to the identity of who, or what, might be waiting for us inside.

'You first,' I said to Jenks.

'Not likely,' he hissed.

'You're thin,' I argued. 'You can scarper quicker.'

'Look,' he replied. 'We don't know who's in there. It might be Fisty. It might be a madman with an axe . . .'

'Quit squabbling, you yellow wallies,' said Barney, lifting the rubbish board from the window and climbing down. 'After me.'

So, that was it. We were going in. And I had so wanted to be a yellow wally.

I turned to Badger and said, 'Been nice knowing you pal.'

He flapped his ears and peed against the wall. I might have been about to die and he couldn't care. I'd always known he was brainless.

Barney's footsteps crunched across the pitch-black cellar and up into the main hallway. I hung close to his enormous bulk, hoping that if anything attacked us, it would get him first. It probably went against the Agent Z

Code of Honour, but the Agent Z Code of Honour suddenly seemed less important than staying alive.

Behind us, Jenks lingered as far back as possible. The hallway showed no signs of other occupants and the lounge door was ajar, just as we always left it. Barney nudged it open with his toe and wandered in.

We waited whilst he fumbled around in the drawers of the table and found the candles. We heard the scratching of a match against its box and the candle was lit. Our shadows wobbled and danced on the walls behind us. We looked around warily.

The room was empty.

Laughing a little on account of our relief, we followed Barney into the middle of the room and glanced at the Crew's belongings, looking for anything out of place. It took us several minutes to notice that the Beverley Sisters' mints had gone.

'Jenks,' I asked, my voice beginning to dry up, 'did you eat. . . ?'

'Not me,' he said.

'Nor me,' added Barney.

I no longer found the old joke about the three furry sisters amusing. I turned to the doorway and half expected to see them standing there, their semi-transparent legs poking out from beneath their ragged grave clothes. I could almost hear their tiny, rasping voices saying, 'Come with us . . . . Yes, come with us . . .'

Barney started laughing softly.

'Your faces!' he chuckled. 'You should *see* your faces.'

'What?' Jenks said indignantly.

'You're white as sheets,' he chortled.

'But the mints!' demanded Jenks. 'What about the mints?'

'Pff!' scoffed Barney. 'Rats? Mice? Birds? Perhaps I ate them and can't remember. Relax, O.K. I'm going to fix myself a can of Coke? Anyone else fancy one?'

I slumped onto the sofa. Barney was right. Someone had been winding us up. Perhaps it was Barney himself. Either way, Jenks and I had got ourselves into a frenzy for nothing, like little kids who think there's a monster under the bed. 'Sure,' I said. 'Chuck us a can.'

The can was in mid-air when I heard the creak. It was only a tiny creak, but it came from directly above our heads. It sounded exactly like the sort of sound someone would make if they were walking across the floorboards in the bedroom.

Time seemed to slow down. My hair stood on end. My hand went limp. The can flew past my hand and clattered to the floor behind the sofa.

'Wassat?' squeaked Jenks.

I froze. Jenks froze. Barney glanced up at the ceiling.

'It's an old house, right?' he shrugged his shoulders. 'Come on. There are creaks all the time here. They've never bothered you before. And now, just because of those stupid notes, you're like jack-in-the-boxes.'

'Maybe . . . maybe . . .' I said, gripping the arms of the sofa and trying to calm down.

Barney looked at us like a long-suffering father and said, 'O.K. If it's going to make you feel any better, let's go up and take a look.'

'No, no, no,' muttered Jenks, his hands fluttering like little birds.

'Yes, yes, yes,' said Barney, taking hold of Jenks' T-shirt and dragging him slowly towards the door. 'I'm not spending the evening with you two acting like this. We are going to sort this thing out once and for all.' With his other hand, he rummaged in one of the cupboard drawers, found another grubby candle and the box of matches, lit the candle and held it out in front of him. 'Come on.'

Not wanting to be left alone, I followed them out into the hall and towards the staircase, wishing that, sometimes, Barney wasn't quite so grown-up about everything.

I began to feel better as we climbed the staircase. At every step, the rotten wood creaked and groaned beneath our feet. Barney was right. We'd forgotten that the place made noises like this all the time. If the wind was up, it sounded like a pirate galleon in a hurricane.

We mounted slowly into the darkness, the flame of Barney's candle guttering and shaking. We looked in the bathroom. It was empty.

We looked in the box-room and jumped when a shadow flitted across the window as we opened the door. But it was only a squirrel which had hopped in through the broken window.

The smaller of the two bedrooms contained a couple of extremely fat spiders, but that was all. Which left only the room above the lounge.

'Right gentlemen,' announced Barney, sweeping away a veil of cobwebs from around the door, 'if the Masked Crusader is in the Command Centre, *this* is where he's going to be.'

He was lingering. I wondered whether he was scared. Perhaps he was. Perhaps, on the other hand, he just wanted to make Jenks and me as frightened as possible before opening the door. He was doing it very well.

'Get on with it,' I said. 'Please.'

'Certainly,' said Barney, 'if everyone is ready?'

'Barney!' I complained.

He placed his hand on the doorknob and sang a little trumpet fanfare. He was enjoying every moment.

At last, with a grand flourish, he swung the door wide open.

Gingerly, the two of us crept into the room behind him. It was difficult to see much. The candle flame was tiny and half the room was obscured by Barney's shadow. Ahead of us we could see the boarded-up window; to the left, the mouldy, mildewed bed; to the right, an old, wooden wardrobe, one, cracked door hanging off its hinges.

'Well, here we are, boys,' announced Barney.

Jenks and I stepped forwards, sticking close to him, peering into the impenetrable gloom and satisfying ourselves that the room was empty.

Which is when the candle was blown out.

'Damn!' said Barney.

'Hey!' whispered Jenks, panicking again. 'Where are you? Where've you gone?'

'Calm down,' I said, irritatedly. 'We're still here, alright?'

'Hang loose,' said Barney, fumbling in his pockets. 'I've got more matches.'

And the door creaked shut behind us.

'Jenks!' I shouted. I couldn't see anything, but guessed he must have made a run for it. It would have been typical of him. 'Come back, you coward!'

'I haven't gone anywhere,' he quailed into my left ear.

'Barney?' I asked. Perhaps it was he who had closed the door. 'What are you playing at?'

'Just wait, O.K.?' he replied, still fumbling for the matches, his voice trembling in a most unBarneyish way. 'And go and open the door again.'

Carefully, I groped my way back to the door and moved my hand over the cobwebs and the mould on the old wood until I found the heavy, brass handle. I turned it and pulled. 'I can't,' I said.

'Pull it,' insisted Barney angrily, 'you great wazzock!'
The door wouldn't move an inch.

'Just light the candle,' I said, 'and quick.'

I heard the rasp of match, a light flared for a second, then went out. Barney found another match and tried again. The match was blown out a second time. 'I don't know how to say this,' he confessed slowly, 'but something very strange is going on here.'

My skin went cold and, one by one, the hairs down my spine stood on end. I wanted to be sick.

After trying, unsuccessfully, to light three more matches, Barney let out a sigh and said, 'I give up. Let's get that door open and get out of here.'

'Yeh,' said Jenks. 'Too right. Let's leg it.'

Stretching out his hand through the darkness, Barney bumped against my shoulder and I guided him to the door. He found the handle and heaved. The door frame wheezed and the rusty latch scraped, but he had no more luck in opening it than I had done.

'Hmph . . .' he said, and the three of us fell into a nervous silence, broken only by Jenks' rapid breathing, which was growing quicker and hoarser by the minute.

And it was at that moment that the Masked Crusader finally introduced himself.

'Welcome!' came a voice from the darkness – a man's voice, very low, very croaky, very slow. 'I'm glad you could make it.'

The voice scared the hell out of me. But it didn't scare me half as much as Jenks' scream. It sounded like someone driving a big nail through the middle of a cat.

116

'I think it would be best if you sat down,' continued the voice.

'Barney?' I whispered idiotically, 'Barney? Barney?'

But Barney said nothing. I heard feet scrape and two bums hit the floor. Already shaky, my legs gave way beneath me and I joined them. Jenks was breathing so fast, now, that he sounded like a small steam engine.

There was an unpleasant silence for too many seconds, then a light came on, temporarily blinding us and forcing us to shut our eyes. And with the light, music – quietly at first, then getting gradually louder.

I opened my eyes. Four, five yards away, the big black silhouette of a tall caped figure loomed over us. The light shone from directly behind him. Of his face and clothing you could see nothing – only the light and the huge black outline of his body.

'Good,' said the voice, 'now we're all sitting comfortably.'

We were not sitting comfortably. Out of the corner of my eye I could see Jenks' lower lip wobbling like a twanged ruler. Barney, on the other side of me, looked as if he had died and been stuffed. The only thing moving on his face were the beads of sweat rolling out of his hair and down his cheek.

'You are probably wondering . . . why I brought you here tonight . . .' the voice continued, breaking into a quiet, self-satisfied chuckle.

The music was sinisterly familiar. I racked my brains but I couldn't remember where I had heard it before. It brought to mind pictures of vast roaring flames.

'I shall tell you in due course,' he said. 'But first . . . let me introduce myself . . .'

I realised that the Masked Crusader had asthma. Between every few words, he would stop and take in a slow and painful draught of breath. It should have made him sound like a weed. On the contrary, it somehow made him super-scary, like someone breathing through an oxygen mask.

'I am . . . the Masked Crusader,' he explained. 'It is my job to . . . keep an eye on certain things . . . . Yes, that is a good way of describing my . . . function.'

The Masked Crusader stepped backwards and sat himself down on an old chair. His boots were enormous and scraped noisily on the old wooden planking.

My guts began to feel hot and squirmy, just like they'd done last year when the entire school came down with food poisoning. But it wasn't salmonella omelettes to blame this time. It was pure fear.

'It is my job to make sure that people . . . behave . . . I make sure that they don't overstep certain . . . boundaries.'

The music was rising to a loud, insistent fanfare. Under the trumpets, you could hear a thumping drum begin to beat.

'And you . . . I am afraid . . . have done just that. You have . . . overstepped certain boundaries . . . You have broken certain rules . . . You have tangled with forces about which you know very little . . . forces more dangerous than you could ever imagine.'

This was all too, too horrible for real life. I started to

hope that I would wake up and find Mum standing at the end of my bed with a cup of coffee in her hands, telling me I'd overslept.

'I am . . . the guardian of those forces. And it pains me to find that you have been . . . trespassing in my world.'

I pinched myself, but didn't wake up.

'I have brought you here tonight to make certain . . . that you never . . . never . . . tangle with these forces again.'

At my side, Jenks' head was nodding in agreement. His lips were forming the words, 'Yes, yes, yes . . .' but no sound was coming out.

'To make sure that you never tangle with these forces again . . . I am going to have to punish you. I trust that you will . . . understand.'

Involuntarily, my hand reached out and held onto Barney's arm for safety.

'Prepare yourselves. . . !' said the voice.

I felt my mouth opening, ready for a really good scream, when, suddenly, to my surprise, I felt myself being whisked off the floor. Not by the Masked Crusader, but by Barney, who had jumped to his feet and was hoiking me upright by my shirt collar.

'Now! Go! Run for it!' he bellowed.

Agent Z Panic-Plan No. 876 had obviously come into instant operation. I found my feet and heard the manic laughter of the Masked Crusader cackling beneath the roaring music.

'You will . . . never . . . be able to . . . escape . . . I will be watching you . . . forever.'

119

'The door!' Barney barked.

We threw ourselves towards the door as one. I stretched out my hand, jerked the knob and found it unexpectedly unlocked. We smacked it aside and tumbled into the pitch-black corridor like three pilots scrambling to parachute from a burning plane.

We went down the rickety staircase in a thrashing mess of legs and arms. A banister snapped. By some miracle, Barney managed to remain underneath for most of the descent and we were not crushed.

After we had come to a halt in the hallway, we lay in the dark, dazed for a few seconds, before untangling our limbs. Upstairs the music and the laughter continued unabated.

Oddly, the first thing that popped into my head was Brenda. I now knew how she must have felt when Jenks had told her about the Beverley Sisters. I felt sorry for having laughed at her. I wouldn't have wished this kind of terror on anyone.

'Move it!' ordered Barney heaving himself upright and spilling us onto the floor on either side of him.

And then another thought struck me.

On second thoughts, I didn't feel sorry for Brenda. She was stupid. The Beverley Sisters didn't exist. Only an idiot would have believed Jenks' ludicrous story. And only a fool would have believed in the Masked Crusader. He was about as real as Father Christmas and the Tooth Fairy.

We didn't know who he was, but he certainly wasn't the guardian of dark and mystic forces. He was just somebody with a big cape, a croaky voice and a grudge against the Crane Grove Crew.

Then, finally, I remembered where the music came from. No wonder it was familiar. It was the music they played over all those old films of the Apollo rockets taking off from Cape Canaveral. Suddenly, it didn't seem sinister any more. The Masked Crusader was getting less and less frightening by the second.

'Come *on*!' insisted Barney, tugging at me as Jenks leapt to his feet and began getting his directions.

'No! Wait!' I snapped, grabbing hold of Jenks' trouser leg. 'You don't believe all that gibberish, do you?'

'Ben . . .' Barney said, slowly, looking at me as if the shock had driven me suddenly insane, 'stand up. Follow me. Let's get out of here.'

'Listen,' I said, still panting from our accidental gymnastics. 'Think about it.' I gripped harder as Jenks started to squeal and pull his leg away from my hand. 'The Masked Crusader doesn't exist. It's someone with a torch and a cassette player and walking boots. It's got to be.'

'Let me *go-o-o-o-o-o*!' Jenks wailed like a baby.

'You're very probably right, Ben,' said Barney, slipping into his hassled-parent role, 'and we can have a very interesting talk about this later, but . . .'

'The key,' I said, as a brainwave hit me. 'The key to all the inside doors. We put it somewhere.'

'Er, in the fridge, Ben . . . but hey. . . !'

I sprinted out of the darkened hallway, stumbled to the fridge and dug the key out of the freezer compartment.

121

We'd found it the day we discovered the Command Centre, sticking out of the bathroom lock. It fitted all the internal doors. I sprinted back into the hallway. 'Right,' I said, 'let's give him a taste of his own medicine. Whoever he is.'

'You're mad,' said Barney, shaking his head.

Perhaps I was. Perhaps the fright had damaged my brain. For whatever reason, I had made up my mind. We were not going to run squealing into the night and let some wheezy bloke in fancy dress make prats of us. Besides, this was *our* place. If we didn't get rid of him right now, it would never be the same again.

'That's it,' said Jenks flatly, turning on his heels. 'I'm going.'

'Go on then, Flannelhead,' said Barney dismissively, waving him away. 'Ben . . . I'm with you.'

Together, we groped our way back up the crumbling stairs, leaving Jenks standing forlornly in the hallway, not knowing whether to follow us, or to remain alone in the dark.

The landing was still illuminated by the bright light spilling from the bedroom, and the Masked Crusader was still laughing, though the chuckles were weaker now, as if he was getting bored of this act.

'Quick,' I said quietly to Barney. 'Before he knows what's hit him.'

'Three. Two. One,' whispered Barney.

We ran at the door, ducked into the room, grabbed the knob, ducked back and heaved it shut. We heard the Masked Crusader leap to his feet and stomp towards us.

Barney hung onto the handle tug-of-war-style, and I wiggled the key into the lock.

'Hurry,' hissed Barney, as unseen hands began to wrestle with the door from the other side.

One quick twist and the lock clicked shut.

'Done,' I said with relief.

We staggered backwards and rested against the nearest mossy wall.

'You . . . You little . . . Wait till . . .' spluttered the Masked Crusader, hammering at the other side of the door, and sounding most unlike a guardian of secret forces.

Barney fumbled in his pocket and lit a match. The thumped door was holding up well.

'Wow!' said Jenks' head as it surfaced gingerly at the top of the stairs. 'You got him.'

'We got him,' I grinned.

'And now?' asked Barney.

'We let him stew,' I said, casually.

It was ten minutes later that we heard him smashing the boards away from the bedroom window.

'He's escaping!' spluttered Jenks, startled by the sudden noise.

'Downstairs!' I ordered, without stopping to wonder what this nameless and angry stranger might decide to do to us when there wasn't a door between us. 'Round the back!'

We flew down the stairs, more gracefully this time, skeltered into the basement and squirmed up through the window recess into the moonlit wood. Skidding on the leaves and twigs, we rounded the house in time to see a tall, caped figure plunge out of the darkness into the bank of mud beneath the back windows.

His outfit, which had looked terrifying in silhouette, looked ridiculous now: walking boots, cycling tights, a stocking mask with eye holes and a tartan rug pinned to his shoulders. It was most certainly not a Superhero's wardrobe.

He didn't have a Superhero's co-ordination, either. He was lying on the ground, rolling around and gripping a twisted ankle, shouting, 'Aaaargh. . . ! Damnation. . . !'

Scenting victory, Barney let out a war whoop and the three of us plunged towards the writhing figure ready to unmask him.

'No!' he growled as he turned and caught sight of us storming through the undergrowth. 'Go away!' He hauled himself to his feet, and headed for the trees.

Diving between the twisty trunks in hot pursuit, Jenks and I had begun to whoop, too. We were gaining on him. It was dark under the trees, and he was limping. It would be a matter of seconds before we caught him.

Turning briefly, he saw us on his heels and let out a small gasp of terror. Grabbing his tartan super cape, he threw it over his face to disguise himself. And ran into a tree.

We lay on the ground laughing so hard, that when we finally got the energy together to take a look around, there was nothing left of the Masked Crusader except a tattered shred of tartan rug clinging to a nearby twig.

It didn't seem to matter. We'd won. That was the important thing.

We continued lying there, on our backs in the darkness, the damp leaves under our heads, for several minutes, like three little stone figures on three little stone tombs in an overgrown graveyard. Looking up, we could see the scruffy net of black branches, and, beyond the branches, the stars.

'Look!' said Barney quietly at one point. 'A comet.'

And so there was. I wiped the tears of laughter from my eyes and saw a miniature ball of orange fire slowly tracing its way across the sky on a long, fine trail of red flame; glowing suddenly more brightly, then disappearing as it entered the atmosphere and was burnt up.

'Mega,' said Jenks.

# Pink, Pink, Pink and More Pink

The evening's excitement wasn't over. We looked at our watches, realised we were in hot water and decided to head home. We stood, brushed the twigs and moss from our jeans, found the hole in the fence and cut across the silent park to the main road.

And there he was. Fisty. Loping home under the street lights, a cigarette hanging from his lips and a tattered Adidas bag slung over his shoulder. In the pandemonium of the last few hours I'd forgotten he existed. Next week was the week he returned to school, a date which had been hanging over the three of us like a suspended axe.

And yet . . . tonight, he seemed just that little bit smaller than usual, just that little bit less terrifying, and we seemed just that little bit bigger, that little bit tougher, that little bit less totally scared out of our wits.

The time was suddenly forgotten. Barney fell to the floor and did a commando roll into the bushes. 'Down, down, down. We have target in our sights. Wilko.'

'Copy,' I said, slipping down beside him and worming my way up the flower border, with Jenks at my heels. 'This is PRG45. Let's move to attack readiness.'

'Tango Charlie,' said Barney. 'We have Betamax. Do you read?'

'I read,' I replied. 'That is affirmative. You have clearance, Delta Niner. I confirm. You have clearance.'

Jenks, unable to think up anything appropriate to say, made radio static noises from somewhere under the rhododendrons.

'Stand by,' added Barney finally, 'All non-combat units pull clear. Weapons lock. Let's take him out.'

Fisty turned at the end of the road and we slipped over the railings. Jenks caught the bum of his jeans on a jagged rivet and landed on the pavement with a loud ripping noise which sounded extremely unprofessional. We ignored him and went into paratrooper crouches behind the postbox.

'Cover me,' said Barney, running along the pavement to the nearest big bush and throwing himself into it.

Unsure what he meant, I sprinted after him anyway and threw myself into the same bush. When Jenks arrived, we repeated the process all over again, leap-frogging down the street from shrub to hedge to shrub. At the end of the street we peered out from the inside of a big privet to catch Fisty's next move.

'My mum is going to kill me,' said Jenks to himself, twisting round to examine the flap of torn denim.

Fisty turned into Wordsworth Road.

'Just out of interest . . .' I asked Barney, trying to sound relaxed and unterrified. 'What are we going to do to Fisty when we catch up with him?'

'Confirm, Betamax. Unit will exterminate target. Repeat. Exterminate target. Till then, maintain radio silence. Close down all channels. Over and out,' Barney replied, mechanically.

Crossing my fingers and hoping he didn't get too carried away with the game and *actually* attempt to exterminate Fisty, I grabbed a privet branch like Barney had done, held it over my face and zig-zagged across the mini-roundabout.

Three junctions later, Fisty turned onto the Webster Estate. It seemed an appropriate place for the Morgans to live. The council had been planning to pull it down for years. Half the flats were burnt out. There were huge spray-painted skull-murals over the walls; and the central courtyard was filled with a huge mountain of rubbish which people in the top flats threw off the balconies: leftovers, dirty nappies, old beds, cookers, that sort of stuff. Most of the cars on the Webster Estate were stolen, and the dogs ate children for breakfast.

I tried not to look at my watch. If Mum knew I was here, at this time of night, Dad would have to bring her round with smelling salts.

'Stay in formation,' said Barney.

We stayed very tightly in formation.

Fisty crossed the main courtyard, stopped next to a rusty, white transit van, then did something rather odd. He turned and looked around the courtyard, checking to see if anyone else was watching him. We stepped back into the shadows by the waste bins, and it occurred to me that, maybe, Fisty didn't live here. Maybe he was about to burgle someone's flat, or pick up a stolen car.

A man came out of the bottom of a staircase, got into a Mercedes and screeched into the night. Fisty waited until he had gone, then disappeared into the gap between Beaumont House and Fletcher House.

We ran after him, keeping an eye out for Rottweilers and falling fridges. We went through the same gap and found ourselves on an empty patch of wasteground surrounded by a wall. Barney made an over-the-top kind of signal and we scrambled up the wall, grunting and panting and trying to look as much like war-hardened commandos as we could.

'Target tracking North-56. Copy,' said Barney as we tumbled onto the grassy slope beyond the wall. Crossing the ring-road, in fact, by the little footbridge.

'Affirmative. We have copy.'

We slithered down through the uncut grass and beetled up the metal steps onto the footbridge. We slipped across, high above the roaring traffic and followed Fisty up the Bridlepath through Pottery Wood until we found ourselves on Magpie Lane. And I thought to myself – he really is going to burgle someone.

There was no other reason for him to be in Magpie Lane. This was Nobsville. These houses had nine bedrooms apiece and tennis courts attached. There were sports cars on the gravel and barbecues at the poolside. If any of the residents caught sight of an oik like Fisty through their velvet curtains, they'd probably call the police – or save time by whisking the shotgun off the rack and driving him away with a few warning shots.

On the other hand, if he was out burgling, he was being a touch casual about it. Still swaggering, he slung his sports bag onto his other shoulder, threw his cigarette away and turned into the drive of Badger's Den, a particularly sumptuous, ivy-covered, half-timbered mansion.

'Target manoeuvring into designated attack area,' whispered Barney and threw his huge bulk over the garden fence in a surprisingly agile way.

'Check.' We tumbled into the shrubbery behind him, flattening a small bed of geraniums.

When Fisty rang the big, echoing doorbell, we were only yards away from him, lying face down on the sticky mud beneath the short, fat fir trees which lined the drive. At any other time, it would have seemed moronically dangerous. But the evening had started out weird and got weirder by the minute. This kind of craziness had come to seem completely normal by now.

'All units hang fire,' muttered Barney into a large pine-cone, 'and give me a recon vector. Let's lock on. Do we have contact?'

The solid, wooden door swung open.

'We have contact,' I confirmed.

Which is when the evening changed rapidly from

weird to hyper-weird.

A large woman in a floral dress, stood looking at Fisty for a few seconds, then screwed up her face as if she was about to burst into tears and threw her arms round his neck.

'Poppet!' she whined. 'Oh, I'm so glad you're back. Your father and I were absolutely worried to death about you. We thought something terrible might have happened. Where have you been, you naughty little sausage?'

Fisty said nothing, just squirmed out of her grasp and dropped his bag.

'Tell Mumsy . . .' the woman continued. 'Tell Mumsy where you've been all this time.'

The heavy door clumped shut.

We lay in shock for a long time before Jenks spluttered, 'But . . . he said . . . he said his father was . . .'

'Shut up!' insisted Barney, 'and give me some peace and quiet. I need to appreciate what has just happened. I want to remember it perfectly for the rest of my life.'

I kept silent for a full minute, but finally I couldn't hold the laughter down any longer. I rolled over onto my back and took a deep breath ready to let rip.

'Oi-oi-oi!' tutted Barney, clamping his chubby hand across my mouth. 'Be careful.'

'Barney,' I said through his fingers, seeing a light come on above me on the first floor. He took his fingers away. 'What do you reckon? Fisty's bedroom?'

The craziness had gone to our heads. Growing next to the front wall of the house was a huge, knobbled oak. We were up it in seconds, like huge, mutant squirrels – Jenks and I manhandling Barney at the tricky bits, pulling his armpits, shoving his buttocks, trying to keep his trainers out of our faces. Somewhere high up in the knotty mess of branches we hit the jackpot.

'I do not believe it,' said Barney, shaking his head. 'I just do not believe it.'

'Where, where, where?' gibbered Jenks.

I gripped his ears and aimed his head in the direction of the lit window. Twenty feet away, behind the glass, Fisty was getting out of his school uniform.

The walls were pink. There were pink flowers on the

duvet. There were flowers on the pink pillow. There were flowers on the little skirt of pink material that ran around the bed. The lamp shade had tassels. The curtains had a fringe.

Fisty had defiantly put a Harley Davidson poster up in the middle of one wall, but it didn't make a lot of difference. The pink and the flowers and the tassels were too overwhelming. They made the Harley Davidson look like a souped-up ladies' shopping trolley.

I suddenly understood why Fisty always left school in the direction of the Webster Estate. I suddenly understood why, half an hour earlier, he had stood at the end of the courtyard and looked back to see whether he was being followed before leaping over the wall and crossing the ring-road.

This was the *Big Secret*. I bet Sharon Mortimer didn't know about this. I bet no-one in the entire school knew about this. Except us. It was like finding a football-sized chunk of twenty-four carat gold lying in the street.

Barney turned to me and held out his hand for shaking. 'Yes, indeed. Mission A-1 total effectiveness recon. Copy. Do you vectorise? I repeat. Do you vectorise?'

'We vectorise,' I said, shaking his hand.

'Roger,' said Jenks.

Which is when the branch underneath us gave way with the sound of a large hand grenade going off. We were spilled onto the ground inside a huge bristly mess of leaves and twigs and acorns and grass.

For some reason, it seemed hilarious. We didn't care. We knew the Big Secret now. We were unstoppable.

Mind you, when Fisty's father stepped out of the front door onto the gravel, bellowing. 'I say! What the devil! Who is that?', we made a point of ducking and diving at high speed down the drive to the main road just in case he did have a shot-gun.

## Eat My Socks

I arrived home four hours late, covered from head to toe in scratches, mud-stains, oak leaves and squashed geranium.

I opened the door and saw Mum coming towards me like a hungry jackal. 'And what kind of time do you call this, eh?'

'Far too late,' I said diplomatically.

A knitting needle waggled alarmingly next to my face for a few seconds, and then, suddenly, Mum couldn't keep it up any longer. Anger was never one of her strong points.

She looked despairingly at my dishevelled clothes. I grinned sheepishly back at her. She ruffled my hair, shook her head, raised her eyebrows, smiled and said, 'Don't tell me, Ben. Let me guess. You were walking home from school when you saw these famous international criminals kidnapping the captain of the local football team and bundling him into this getaway biplane and you chased after them and hung onto the wheels and you were dragged through this field while they took off and they flew for hundreds of miles with you hanging onto the undercarriage and finally . . . Am I close?'

Mum was in one of her ultra-good moods. I slumped down beside her on the other kitchen chair. 'No. Nothing like that at all. But it was a great story. You've got a real talent there.'

'Thank you. Fancy a mug of hot chocolate?'

One of her hyper-ultra-mega-good moods.

'Fab,' I said.

Badger shuffled up, slid his head into my lap and breathed at me. 'Ah . . .' I said, suddenly remembering. 'Badger.'

'Quite,' said Mum, pouring the milk into the saucepan. 'You can't get rid of him that easily, I'm afraid, Ben. Mrs Capaldi from the chippie found him rifling through their waste bins and brought him over.' She lit the gas. 'So?'

'So?'

'What happened tonight?'

'Oh, right. Tonight. Well, it was *almost* as unbelievable as the kidnap stuff.'

'Tell me,' she said, excavating the hot chocolate tin from the back of the cupboard. 'Your father' gone to the All-Night Elvis Film Festival at the Ritzy with a couple of cronies, and I've got Turkish past participles coming out of my ears. I could do with a bit of light entertainment. Chuck your clothes in the washing machine, get your jim-jams on, then we can both put our feet up and you can tell me the whole thing. Right from the beginning.'

So I told her. Everything. Right from the beginning. The Beverley Sisters, the clingfilm, the incredible flying potato, the kippers, the Masked Crusader, the tartan cape, the pink bedspread etc., etc., etc. I left out a few bits of ultra-classified Agent Z information, like the location of the Command Centre, the secret codes and stuff, but she got the rest of the story in glorious technicolour.

We were well into the small hours by the time I had ground to a halt.

'God. . . !' sighed Mum, slumping back onto the sofa. 'What it is to be young.' She leaned over and slipped the liqueur chocolates off the coffee table. 'Why don't I ever have evenings like that?'

'No problem,' I said. 'Get kitted out in your gardening clothes tomorrow and we'll do an undercover commando trek across the ringroad to Fisty's place. Chuck a stink bomb through his bedroom window or something.'

'It's a nice offer, but I don't think it's quite my style, Ben. Perhaps I'd better stick to being old and boring, if that's alright by you. Have a liqueur chocolate, by the way. Then you'd best scoot upstairs and into bed before you father gets home or we'll both be in trouble.'

'Affirmative,' I leant over and took a miniature chocolate barrel out of the box. 'Nutrition-docking imminent. Wilko. We have a Grand Marnier. Repeat. We

137

have a Grand Marnier. End of transmission. Over and out.'

'Night, love.'

'Night, Mum.'

Dad came into the kitchen when I was finishing off my bowl of cereal. Mum had obviously told him the whole story when he got in. From the look in his eyes, he hadn't believed a word of it. Humming some unidentifiable rock and roll tune, he shimmied over to the cooker and slid two pieces of bread under the grill.

'The Masked Crusader?' he chuckled. 'Agent Z? The Command Centre?' He gave me an I-know-what-you're-up-to kind of wink. 'I reckon you're having your mother on. I reckon you're up to something.' He tapped the side of his nose. 'Either that or you've gone stark-staring bonkers.' Dad looked as if he was in a mickey-taking mood. I wasn't going to convince him, so I didn't bother.

'You're right, Dad. I was having her on,' I said, rinsing my empty bowl, slipping it into the rack and picking up my gym bag.

'Uh?' he replied, taking his toast out from under the grill.

'It was a cover,' I explained. 'Barney, Jenks and I were

robbing a bank. We do it every weekend. Last night we got a bit held up in this rather sticky shoot-out.' Dad's jaw hung open for a few seconds. I whisked a piece of toast from his hand and slid out of the door. 'Catch you later.'

'Oi!' came a distant shout as I disappeared out of the garden gate.

There were a couple of surprises in store at school. The first was for Fisty.

The three of us met up next to the games shed and agreed tactics. Barney was to do the talking. Jenks and I would stand there and look tough. Every time we got nervous we reminded ourselves of the fringes and the tassles. It was going to be alright. It really was going to be alright. 'Trust me,' Barney had said, and we almost did. 'Talk of the devil,' Barney smiled, nodding across the playground, 'and just on time, too.'

We took deep breaths and, together, the three of us strode as manfully as we could towards the loping ape. Which threw him for a start.

Fisty was used to people running away from him; and fast. If people casually sauntered towards him, especially smaller people, especially people he wanted to kill, then they'd probably gone insane.

He turned in our direction and spat lazily onto the tarmac. 'I'm amazed that you little slimebags dare show your faces round here . . .' He cracked his knuckles. '. . . on *my* patch. Well, let me give you a bit of advice for free . . .'

'Shut it,' said Barney, bluntly, 'and let me give *you* a bit of advice.'

I felt dizzy hearing Barney say it. It was getting to the very top of the big dipper, pausing and suddenly having the carriage fall away underneath you as you plunged over the edge. Fisty was speechless.

Barney carried on, 'What would you say if I was to say to you . . . "Badger's Den", for example?' He paused, letting it sink in. Fisty narrowed his eyes and looked poisonously round at the three of us, like a trapped rat. 'Or "Magpie Lane"? In fact, what would you say if I was to say to you . . .' Barney switched smoothly into a convincing imitation of Fisty's mum. '"Oh, I'm so glad you're back, Poppet. Your father and I were absolutely worried to death about you. We thought something terrible might have happened. Where have you been, you naughty little sausage? Tell Mumsy"."

Fisty was hotching from one foot to the other. His hands were clenched. His teeth were clenched. His forehead was clenched. He looked as if he were on the verge of exploding.

'Actually, I think pink is a very fetching colour for a bedroom,' added Barney, delicately scraping a piece of dirt from under his nails.

'You . . . you. . .you. . .' Fisty was almost too angry to speak. 'You scum. You total, stinking, toilet-scum. You scummy, little, stinking . . .'

'Yes, yes, yes,' said Barney wearily. 'That's all very well. However, I just wanted to say . . .'

Fisty's hands stretched out automatically towards Barney's neck, as if to strangle him. Barney coolly waggled his finger and tutted. Fisty realised that it would be an exceedingly stupid move and retracted his hands.

'I just wanted to say,' Barney repeated, 'that we haven't told anyone about this. Not a soul. And I don't think there's any reason why we should.' He turned to each of us in turn. 'Is there?'

'No,' I said.

'Nope,' agreed Jenks.

'Of course,' said Barney, casually rootling in his ear with his little finger, 'you have to be nice to us. In fact, you have to be *very* nice. But I don't see that that will be a problem. Do you?'

If you looked very closely you could almost see the steam coming out of Fisty's nostrils. He fought to bring himself under control, then hissed, slowly, 'If you tell *anyone*. And I mean *anyone*. If you tell a single, stinking, scummy person, I'll . . . I'll . . .'

Behind me, Jenks was fishing something out of his bag.

'We won't tell a dicky bird,' explained Barney politely. 'All you have to do is treat us with a little bit of respect. A little bit of dignity. A little bit of consideration.'

Jenks stepped forward with a huge grin on his face, holding out a handful of vile, muddy rags. 'You also have to eat my games socks.'

The second suprise was for us.

The first lesson was history with Mr Forsyth. We'd moved on from the Vikings. We were doing the Normans now, and I knew as much about the Normans as I did about Turkish past participles. In the excitement of the weekend, I'd also forgotten to read the book we'd been given for homework. I was steeling myself for a tough forty minutes.

As it turned out, I didn't give the Normans another thought for the entire lesson. And I didn't need to, on account of the fact that Forsyth came into the room limping, and with a nasty-looking bruise smack in the middle of his forehead. Barney, Jenks and I exchanged shocked, knowing glances, and everything fell suddenly into place.

Forsyth was the Masked Crusader. It was revenge for the kippers. It explained why the man in the tartan cape wanted to hide his face so badly. As one, Barney, Jenks and I turned towards the front of the classroom, our jaws hanging as far open as they would have done had Forsyth wandered into the room naked.

'1066 is the one date that everybody knows,' he began, putting his briefcase down, taking off his jacket and pinning up a big poster of something apparently called the Bayeux Tapestry, 'and with good reason. 1066 is perhaps the most important date in the whole of English history. Now, when the army of William, Duke of Normandy, beat the English army of Harold at the Battle of Hastings . . .'

It didn't matter that I hadn't a clue what he was talking about. It didn't matter that I hadn't read the book. Forsyth took no notice of us whatsoever. He didn't catch our eyes. He didn't ask us a single question. It was as if Barney, Jenks and I had become invisible.

'Right. That's your lot,' said Forsyth as the bell rang for the end of the lesson, and everyone plunged towards the door.

Except Barney, Jenks and I. After thirty seconds there

was only us three and Forsyth left in the room. For some inexplicable reason, we felt glued to our seats. We were waiting for something; waiting for some kind of explanation; for some kind of revelation.

Slowly, Forsyth stood, slipped his jacket back on, picked up his briefcase and walked towards us. He was not smiling. His face looked totally blank. I hadn't a clue what was coming. An apology? Congratulations? Detentions? Expulsion?

He stopped a little way in front of us and sucked his teeth for a few moments before saying. 'Well, gentlemen; I think we'd better call it quits, don't you?'

Barney, who was good at these kind of complicated grown-up situations said, 'You're right. Let's call it quits.'

'Good,' agreed Forsyth bluntly.

143

And with that he turned gingerly on his twisted ankle, and marched as swiftly as he could out of the room.

'That is one *ugly* creature,' Barney grimaced, pressing his face to the glass of Presley's tank.

'He's not meant to be beautiful,' I answered. 'He's an African toad. They're *meant* to be ugly. It's camouflage. Besides, he's ill and we're taking him to the vet tomorrow evening, so don't go poking him about, O.K.?'

We were sitting in my bedroom. Mum was downstairs cooking us lasagne, and we were discussing the Forsyth Puzzle. Me, I was still confused. I could still hardly believe he was the Masked Crusader. He was such a dry old stick, usually, and it was such a whacky thing to do. And what was all this 'quits' stuff? Why was he so keen to keep the whole thing so quiet? Did he think he'd get into trouble? Perhaps he was embarrassed. But about what? About being beaten by three puny kids? About being seen wearing a tartan cape and cycling tights? About having a sense of humour?

Added to which, he must have seen our noticeboard in the Command Centre. You couldn't miss it. He must know all about the clingfilm and the atom-parcel and the Z-potato – but he was saying nothing. Very strange.

Jenks, on the other hand, wasn't puzzled at all. Jenks was furious. The Masked Crusader, it seemed, had spooked him good and proper. 'He must have spied on us . . . with a telescope or binoculars or something . . . like, to see where the Command Centre was. He must have been watching us for weeks. Then he broke in . . . to *our* place . . . and then he scared the living daylights out of us. I mean . . . I mean he could have given us heart attacks. Then it wouldn't have been so funny, would it?'

'I'm beginning to wish he had given you a heart attack,' said Barney sarcastically. 'Just give it a rest, will you?' He turned to me. 'How long does your Mum's lasagne take, Ben? I could eat a horse.'

As if by magic, there was a knock on the door, it swung open and Dad's head appeared. 'Sorry for upsetting the meeting, gentlemen,' he said, 'but supper is served. If you would like to make your way down to the dining room.'

I told Dad about the Forsyth puzzle between mouthfuls of lasagne. '. . . and Jenks is angry because he scared us so much. And I'm just confused. I mean, I just can't work Forsyth out at all.'

Dad chewed thoughtfully for a few seconds before chuckling and saying. 'Well he sounds like a pretty cool dude to me.'

'Dad!' I cringed.

It had been bad enough listening to him singing Elvis songs downstairs while we were lying around upstairs earlier in the evening, but having him say 'cool dude' in front of my friends was the pits.

'And what if he did scare the pants off you?' Dad

145

continued. 'Sounds like you've been getting up everyone else's noses all term. I don't think you've got a leg to stand on.'

I was still blushing visibly.

Barney wagged a slice of over-buttered bread at me. 'No, Ben, I reckon your Dad's right. Forsyth's a cool dude. That's all there is to it. We got one over on him. He got one over on us . . . almost. And now we're quits. We're all cool dudes. It's simple.'

'You see,' Dad said, turning to me, 'I may be a hundred and seven, but I'm not totally senile yet.'

'Would you like fifths?' Mum asked Barney, noticing his empty plate.

'Absolutely,' said Barney, licking his lips in anticipation. 'Mrs Hurst, I have to say, you cook like a dream.'

So, next lunch time, we met up in the entrance hall and made our way to the staff room. We stood outside, straightening our ties and brushing the crisp-crumbs off our jackets, then knocked.

Mrs Phelps answered the door. 'Hello Ben,' she smiled, 'what can I do for you?'

'We'd like a word with Mr Forsyth, if that's O.K.?' I replied.

'Sure,' she said. 'How's the leg by the way?'

'Oh, the leg,' I said, suddenly remembering. I bent down and rubbed my right kneecap. 'Not too bad.'

'So the other one's gone now, then?' she asked.

'Er . . . yes,' I said, rubbing both kneecaps. 'Just have to keep a brave face on it, you know.'

'You poor old thing . . .' she sighed, shaking her head. 'Anyway, just hang on there for a few seconds and I'll go and dig him out for you.' She turned and disappeared into the depths of the room.

'What's wrong with your knees?' asked Jenks, puzzled.

'I'll explain later,' I said.

'Ah . . . you lot,' said Mr Forsyth, appearing in the doorway.

'Hello, Sir,' I said.

'Well?' he asked.

'We'd like to have a word with you, Sir,' said Barney, in a very businesslike manner, 'if you have a few minutes to spare, that is.'

'Certainly,' he said, hunting for somewhere to deposit his coffee cup. 'Is this the sort of word we can have in the corridor, or do we need to retire to the library for a bit of privacy?'

'The library,' said Barney. 'If that's no problem.'

'No problem whatsoever,' he said, matter-of-factly.

'Fire away then,' Forsyth said, seating himself on one of the book trolleys.

'Ben?' said Barney. 'Would you like to do the honours?'

'O.K.' I said, clearing my throat. 'Mr Forsyth, we . . . the three of us . . . would like you to have one of these.' I dug around in my jacket pocket, pulled out a Z badge and handed it to him.

'You have to wear it on the inside of your lapel so that no-one else can see it,' said Jenks, turning back his lapel and showing his own Z badge. 'It's like a sort of, you know, honorary membership.'

'For outstanding bravery,' I said.

'And being a good laugh,' added Jenks.

'And for being a cool dude,' Barney concluded.

Forsyth turned the badge over in his hands, inspected it closely, then said, 'Well . . . this is a bit of a turn-up for the books. ''A cool dude''!' he chuckled, shaking his head. Turning his lapel over, he pinned the Z badge to the reverse.

We kept our mouths shut. If the truth be told, Jenks and I wanted to ask him exactly how he had done it: how he had known about the kippers; how he had set the whole thing up; why he hadn't turned us in, etc., etc., etc. But, as Barney said, we were members of the Cool Dude Crew, now, and members of the Cool Dude Crew had to be laid back about these things.

Forsyth stood up, gave us a large wink, then turned and made his way back towards the staff room, chuckling quietly to himself, his Z badge secreted under his lapel.

# Going Down in Flames

The vet said that Presley had been dead for about three weeks.

I was sad for a day or so, but I got over it. I asked Dad if we could have him stuffed. As I explained, he wouldn't look any different and we'd save a lot of money on cat food. Dad made a few phone calls but with no success. Stuffing a toad was an expensive job – too expensive.

Instead, we decided on a Viking funeral. Dad knocked up a brilliant model longship out of old bits of plywood in the garage. I painted it black and made a cardboard eagle's head to stick on the prow. We wrapped Presley in an old muslin cloth that Mum once used for making Christmas puddings and we laid him out on the deck.

On Saturday evening, Barney, Jenks, Mum, Dad,

Badger and I took him along to the duck pond in Crane Grove Park. Dad poured some paraffin over the boat, put a match to it and pushed it out into the water under the darkening sky. It felt like we were on the gravel beach of a fjord in Norway in 850 AD.

150

We stood in silence as the blazing boat drifted out into the centre of the pond, lighting up the trees around the bank. We remained standing there, our heads bowed, saying our last, silent goodbyes until the flames finally died out and the boat sank.

It was a cool way to go.

# AGENT Z GOES WILD
## by Mark Haddon

*His timing was perfect. He had taken the top
off his athlete's foot cream, squeezed
a couple of centimetres of it into the
toothpaste, replaced both caps and gathered up
his stuff before either of them had
turned round. 'Come on,' he said to us.
'Let's hit breakfast.'*

Meet Agent Z, whose mission is to wreak
hilarious havoc on the unsuspecting and the
downright deserving, ably assisted in his battle
against boredom by the Crane Grove Crew:
Ben, Barney and Jenks.

A school trip turns to chaos and the Crane
Grove Crew turn detective!

A wildly witty adventure from the author of
*The Curious Incident of the Dog in
the Night-Time.*

0 09 940073 1

**RED FOX**

# THE CURIOUS INCIDENT OF THE DOG IN THE NIGHT-TIME
## *by Mark Haddon*

Fifteen-year-old Christopher has Asperger's Syndrome, a form of autism. He has a photographic memory. He understands maths. He understands science. What he can't understand are other human beings.

When he finds his neighbour's dog, Wellington, lying dead on a neighbour's lawn, he decides to track down the killer and write a murder mystery novel about it. In doing so, however, he uncovers other mysteries that threaten to bring his whole world crashing down around him.

*The Curious Incident of the Dog in the Night-Time* is an astonishing novel – funny, sad and utterly unputdownable.

0 09 945676 1

DEFIΠITIOΠS